IMPOSSIBLE TO FORGET

BY
SALLY HEYWOOD

D1198067

MILLS & BOON LIMITED
ETON HOUSE   18–24 PARADISE ROAD
RICHMOND   SURREY   TW9 1SR

First published in Great Britain 1987
by Mills & Boon Limited

© Sally Heywood 1987

Australian copyright 1987
Philippine copyright 1988
This edition 1988

ISBN 0 263 75901 6

Set in Plantin 10 on 11 pt.
01-0288-52062

Computer typeset by SB Datagraphics,
Colchester, Essex

Printed and bound in Great Britain by
Collins, Glasgow

CHAPTER ONE

'BUZZ me the minute Keith brings the car round to the front, Susie, will you?'

'Will do, boss,' came the jaunty reply over the intercom.

Claudia smiled. Her assistant could be guaranteed to be unflappable, even when the company was presented with the prospect of a meeting like the one that faced them this morning. Make or break time!

To calm her nervous flutters, Claudia allowed herself a leisurely glance in the mirror that hung behind the door of her office suite, while she waited for the car to fetch her. As boss of a beauty clinic in this elegant English spa town, she was thoroughly familiar with the signs of strain that could show up on the face of a twenty-nine-year-old. But the face that gazed back at her from the oval mirror seemed surprisingly calm and untouched by worry lines. Self-discipline and the ability to relax at will seemed to pay off. Come on, though, Keith, she fretted, let's get cracking!

Half an hour with a make-up kit had given her the glossy allure of a movie star. Not that she was bad-looking underneath—her large eyes, an arresting shade of cobalt, hijacked attention even without the professional make-up job she had given them—but she had long ago acquired the habit of covering up the girl from the past beneath a veneer of hard-headed glamour. And today was special.

Flicking back her jet-dark hair from off the shoulders of a powder-blue two-piece, she moved over to her white

5

and gold Regency-style desk. It was immaculately tidy. Once again she checked her briefcase. Keith had all the detailed figures and she had fixed the salient points in her head, so the expensive-looking black Samsonite case was nothing but a stage prop—one she deemed necessary for the image of a successful businesswoman she was hoping to project. She smiled grimly, wondering if this latest gamble meant she was beginning to fool even herself. Power, success—looking at her, she seemed to have both, with more to come if things went her way this morning. If people could only see beneath the cleverly painted exterior . . .

'He's here, Claudia!' crackled the voice over the intercom.

'OK, I'm coming down. Sure you can handle everything?'

'Who? Me?'

Claudia snapped the switch down and made for the door. When she appeared in the softly carpeted peach and gold reception area Susie was nonchalantly watering the baby palm beside her glass-topped desk, but she raised her sleek blonde head as Claudia strode briskly towards the door.

'Sock it to them, Claudia,' she called, adding, 'One look at you and they'll be eating out of your hand!'

'I certainly hope so.' As a one-third owner of the business, Susie's interest was practical as well as personal. In the early days she and Claudia had done all the treatments themselves. Now they had a staff of six, not including several part-timers who ran classes on the exercise side of the business. Working with Claudia for the last five years, Susie could detect signs of strain invisible to other people.

'They'll only have to look at you to realise this outfit is the hotest thing to hit the beauty circuit since—time when,' she reassured.

'I'm not overdoing the glitz and gloss, am I, love? I've got to look serious, too.'

'Call yourself Alexis—these days you don't have to look like one of the chaps to do business with them on an equal footing.'

'Well, let's hope you're right. I'm just not sure what they'll be expecting.'

Conscious of her accountant waiting in the car on the double lines outside the salon, she was about to give a little wave as she left, when her hand flew to her mouth. 'Oh, I forgot to ask. Did Toby ring through the numbers he was inviting to the barbecue next weekend?'

'He did indeed. Want to see his list?'

'I'll look at it later. Bye, love.'

She let herself out through the smoky plate-glass entrance doors that always kept the reception area flatteringly dim. Sun bounced off the paving flags and off the white saloon that waited for her. On seeing her emerge, Keith came swiftly round the front of the car to let her in.

'You look sensational, Claudia!' he exclaimed, giving her arm a quick pat as he slid into the driver's seat.

'Thank you, Keith,' she replied, surprised that he had actually noticed that she'd gone to any trouble. Usually so immersed in his work, he scarcely seemed to register the day-to-day matters that occupied the thoughts of more ordinary mortals. As he urged the car into the passing stream of traffic she turned to him. 'You're looking pretty chic yourself,' she teased. 'Think we'll pull this deal off?'

He drew his lips back briefly behind the crisp reddish-brown beard, and his tone was light, inspiring her with confidence. 'Claudia, if they don't see a good thing coming, they're not the company we're looking for.'

'Groucho Marx—"I don't wanna be a member of a club that has me in it." Very philosophical. I like it,' she replied, curving her lips in a brief smile.

'Keith, do you realise the basis of this whole meeting depends on a single theory?' she mused, as they sped along the high street towards the ring road.

'What's that, Claudia?' he asked, not taking his eyes off the traffic.

'That a company which isn't expanding is stagnating,' she told him. 'I read it in a book somewhere. It must have stuck.'

'I prefer to think that the launch of Claudia Gray into the big time is due to the fact that we're opening up a market nobody else happens to have thought of before.' He changed down and drummed his fingers impatiently as they idled towards a set of red lights. 'Look at how you started. First working in a small salon for somebody else. Then acquiring your own tiny place. You haven't just sat back and watched your business grow, Claudia, you've been constantly looking for new treatments, new products to offer your clients. It's nothing to do with theory. It's because you're an eminently practical woman.'

'Hm.' Compliments made her blush. 'Be that as it may, I'm stuck now, unless I can get out of that sardine can we call a beauty clinic,' she told him. 'Central it may be, but we're bursting at the seams, and that's without the extra sauna and solarium I want to put in.'

'Don't worry. Franchising the Claudia Gray Salon will make you a wealthy woman, and these last few months when you've been searching for bigger premises will seem like a bad dream.'

'I couldn't have done it without you, Keith. Forcing me to restructure the business side of things. I'd coasted on luck and intuition too long.'

'Luck still has a part to play. If the Country House Hotel chain hadn't moved into the area, you'd still be restructuring instead of moving on and up.'

She laughed. 'Country House certainly put a few noses out of joint when they bought Normanby Hall. A white elephant, everybody called it!'

'That's because it had been empty for years.'

'But it was obvious that under the cobwebs and broken gutters it was a beautiful and elegant Georgian mansion, ripe for development.'

'Obvious to you, Claudia, perhaps——'

She snorted at the short-sightedness of the local business community. The hotel chain had quickly turned it into a thriving venue for the well heeled house-party brigade, and the place was thronged with people who seemed willing to pay handsomely for the sybaritic pleasures of country-house living. Each room, she'd been told, was like something out of *Style and Interiors*.

'It was certainly a shot in the dark to approach them with my little package,' she said complacently, as the car lurched forward on to a roundabout, narrowly missing the back end of a bus. 'If Susie hadn't been so enthusiastic when I tested the idea on her first, I would never have had the nerve to go on. I suppose it used to be a thirst for security that drove me in the beginning. Now it's more like curiosity—to see how far I can go. You've been brilliant with the figure work, Keith.' He had backed her up by producing a detailed set of projections that gave her crazy inspiration the air of something concrete and very possible. It was these figures bolstering the proposal that they were now going to lay before the management team from the hotel chain.

Keith swung the car carefully into the gravelled drive, and proceeded with the trepidation of a man on the brink of a date with destiny towards the hotel.

'Don't be down-hearted if we don't get a firm commitment at this stage,' he warned. 'All we need is a foot in the door.'

Claudia's eyes shone. She had a more all-or-nothing attitude to the meeting. If she hadn't, she would probably be an accountant like Keith. His air of caution only served to brace her for the fight. When she stepped through the door into the conference room a few minutes later, there was a smile of success already curving her strawberry-pink lips.

'Mrs Gray, let me introduce you to our chief, Daniel Sinnington,' offered a voice at her shoulder. Her glance flashed briefly along the row of men in dark business suits that confronted her. Then her mouth dropped in astonishment as her glance wheeled back to one face. She felt a nudge from behind as Keith bumped into her with the files then, robotlike, she managed to propel herself into the middle of the room. The sudden sickening panic she felt was, of course, nothing to do with the fact that she was the only woman present. Instead it was the jolt of recognition that flashed between herself and the man whose too-familiar name had just been announced.

Daniel's cool, silver gaze bored into hers across the mirrored expanse of the conference table. He seemed equally startled, the politely welcoming smile fading from his features like a film in slow motion, leaving a cool, distancing manner that exactly matched her own.

'Pleased to meet you, Mr Sinnington,' she murmured, as her thoughts wove a silent scream around the words.

'It's been a long time,' he replied. Then, suddenly, he pulled the remembered lips back in a brief, dazzling smile that smashed at once through all her composure. It seemed as if an unreal silence had fallen over the room as the bombshell of their meeting exploded endlessly between them.

So this was the boss. How unlucky could she get?

Even as she decided that she would go through the motions of discussing the project, then give in to her instinct to run and run from the danger this man embodied, Keith was already pulling her chair back for her. Automatically she found herself sinking into it, fingers trembling at the catch of her briefcase and drawing from it the proposal that had seemed to offer so much. After the meeting, when a day or two had elapsed, and if things had swung their way—she smiled bitterly, head bent over the file—she would tender a definite refusal.

There was *no* way she could ever work with Daniel Sinnington. Not if he was the last man on earth!

The meeting seemed to pass off in a dream. Throughout the discussions she was unable to take her eyes off Daniel, and unable to look him in the eye, either. It was a nerve-fraying cat-and-mouse exercise.

He was still irresistibly attractive. Different to the heart-throb of eighteen, because now he was in his prime. Tall, lithe, muscular as ever—what was he now, thirty? Thirty-one? If nothing else, she would have recognised him by his eyes: they were unusually light grey, bright and alive, just as she always remembered them. Even sitting here in his dark business suit, he looked as if he'd just thrashed an opponent on the squash court. And that hair! It still flopped over one eye as it always had done, blond, outrageous.

She shivered, wondering if he had changed as much as she had, in ways that weren't visible to the naked eye? She had changed, herself, out of all recognition, despite his instant acknowledgement as she'd walked into the room; the changes had been inside, in her soul, where it mattered most. And he had been the one who had caused them.

With a jolt, she realised the meeting was over. Judging by the smiles all round, she and Keith had put their case brilliantly.

'Mrs Gray!' Daniel was coming towards her. There was no escape. he reached out to take her hand. 'Claudia . . .'

How could anyone imbue a mere name with such layers of eroticism? she asked herself. Her heart leap-frogged uncomfortably as he clasped her hand in his. His touch seemed to sting her and she tried to step back, but he was smiling down at her as if oblivious to her mounting panic.

'I suppose it's stating the obvious to say that this is a great surprise,' she got in first, trying to sound casual. There was a dry constriction in her throat that made her voice sound unexpectedly husky. With a start, she heard the door click shut behind her, leaving them alone together. Her startled widening of cobalt eyes brought a humorous quirk to Daniel's mouth.

'Claudia Gray . . . It's less of a mouthful than Claudia de Wend Hampshire, anyway. Did you choose your husband with that in mind, Mrs Gray?'

His silver glance flicked lazily here and there, touching almost finger-light on her face, her hair, and more intimately over the slim, taut, well exercised body in its smart blue suit, and down as far as the trim ankles, the narrow feet encased in elegant matching court shoes. When his glance lazily flicked back to her face after this brief, visual appraisal, the smile she remembered so clearly was still lighting up that disconcerting pair of eyes. He seemed to approve what he saw, and she watched as if mesmerised as he settled his athletic frame on the edge of the polished conference table, dark suit only serving to emphasise the less than discreet physique of a man who had always been as much athlete as scholar. The arrow-sharp agility of the one-time schoolboy boxing champion was still, she noted, much in evidence. It made her long to reach out to him, but instead, rather sharply, she asked, 'You remember me, then?'

'Remember you?' His tone was full of nuance, as if to say, 'How could I ever forget?' and she recalled, with the shock of forgotten memory, the easy charm that had once before devastated her defences.

Now, forewarned, she bent to scoop up her things, saying, 'I'd love to stay and reminisce, but I must get back to the salon.'

'Already? Why the hurry, Mrs Gray?'

It was unfair, the intimate depth to which his voice could sink, giving the simplest question suggestive overtones that made her pulses quicken. Smiling sweetly, she told him, 'I'm a busy woman, Daniel.'

'Not too busy to share a drink for old times, surely?'

'I have to get back——' she repeated stubbornly, and with less composure than before. Her mind was bereft of any more plausible excuse and, as she expected, he tried to sweep her refusal to one side.

'You've done an admirable job this morning, you and your Mr Wilson. Surely you can treat yourself to a short break——'

'I never mix business with pleasure,' she cut in revealingly, turning so sharply towards the door that her hair fanned out like black silk, momentarily screening her pale face from sight. By the time she reached the door he was already there ahead of her.

'Claudia, please! It's like meeting a ghost from the past—when you walked in I almost leapt across the table.' He gave a sudden boyish grin that awakened long-repressed emotions, ones she had forgotten she had ever experienced.

A softness that was now foreign to her threatened to take her in its grip before she recovered sufficiently to clip back, 'Ghost is probably right, and I'm not the type to be haunted by them. It was a long time ago, Daniel, and you're the last person I ever expected to meet——'

'I hope you don't imagine it's going to be the last time,' he replied, undeterred by her less than friendly manner. 'You won't refuse the occasional business lunch with me?' He queried wickedly.

'There may not be any business to discuss,' she countered.

'I'm sure we'll find plenty, once this show's on the road,' he came back quickly.

'It may not reach that stage,' she told him, giving him a careful look. 'This was, as I understand it, an exploratory meeting, and I'm not in a position to discuss company decisions with you before speaking to my accountant——'

'Of course not. I understand that,' he broke in, taking her words at face value,' but later, when the action really starts——'

'No, Daniel. I—look . . .' She searched wildly for the words that would put an end to the sweet torture of talking to him. 'I simply have to go now.'

'You can't be *so* busy——' His eyes were ocean grey as it seemed to reach him that she was less than delighted to see him. 'Pop into the bar for five minutes on your way down—with your accountant as well, of course, and we'll——' His smile returned, inviting an acceptance from her that she had to fight to withhold. Before she knew what he was doing he was ushering her towards the door, the touch of his hand, lodged firmly in the small of her back, bringing with it an erotic pulse of excitement for which she was quite unprepared. With a start, she stepped back out of arm's reach, the dismay on her face betraying the fact that all her defences had crumbled at once.

'Look, Daniel, the past is past,' she snapped before she could allow herself to succumb. 'I'm a different person from the one you used to know. We're strangers now.'

A look of surprise scudded over his face at her cold, matter-of-fact statement, and she suspected that if he had been unsure how to react on first seeing her he was now equally uncertain that to play the scene for golden memories was the right thing, either. It didn't seem to have occurred to him that the memory of their last meeting lingered in anything but a golden glow for her, and now he seemed at a loss as to how to respond.

'You've cut your hair,' he observed inconsequentially.

'In over a decade? Frequently, once a fortnight,' she retorted.

'Why are you fighting me?'

'What?' Her voice was deliberately scathing as she fought his attempt to establish a more personal tone.

'No Ophelia locks, dripping diamonds from the lake.'

The words were so soft she had to strain to catch them, and when she realised what he had said she stared at him in horror. 'Daniel, stop this nonsense! I'm not in the mood to wallow in the past. I've forgotten that horrible time. I'm not the girl you knew. Heavens! We were children, for goodness' sake——'

'If we were, we were very naughty children,' he murmured drily.

She stepped back, her face draining of colour, fumbling for the catch of the door behind her back in order to speed her escape, but he moved forward, reaching out behind her to pull the door open, stepping aside to let her through, then pulling it hard behind them as they moved out into the corridor. Giving her a puzzled frown, he led her rapidly down to the entrance hall, where the others were still chatting amiably to each other. To her surprise, he made no further attempt to detain her, and all she could think was that if she could only get out, away from this reminder of a time she would rather forget, and, more importantly, away from the unsuspecting cause of all the intervening years of heartache, she would survive to fight another day.

Yanking Keith from out of his group in mid-sentence on her way out, she paced agitatedly up and down beside the car while he fumbled interminably with the door-keys. Daniel had come as far as the entrance and, after briefly shaking hands with both of them, disappeared back inside the hotel without any further offer of hospitality. Claudia felt a wave of nausea. His obvious pleasure at seeing her made her feel terrible, as if she was in the wrong to want to punish him—almost as if he were the innocent party in what had happened. It reawakened all the old sense of injustice that she had thought was safely buried. It reawakened her blind anger that she felt proud to think she had grown out of. And it reawakened other feelings that she shuddered to name.

On the drive back to town, Keith's flat, dry voice, calculating profit and loss of a more tangible kind, was getting on her nerves and she had to keep a tight hold on herself in order to refrain from screaming at him to shut up. As soon as he braked outside the salon she flung herself out of the car and left him to park it by himself round the back of the building. Then, with the feeling that she'd just returned from an excursion to another planet, she stumbled back inside the reassuringly familiar foyer. Susie whizzed round the side of her desk as soon as she made her appearance.

'Well? Any good?' Her bright glance darkened as soon as she caught sight of Claudia's set expression. 'Oh, dear. No go, eh? Never mind, love. It's basically a fantastic idea. Somebody'll bite soon enough——'

But Claudia cut off her mistaken assumptions with a shake of her head.

'What on earth's happened?' Susie had been Claudia's second-in-command long enough to recognise that something was wrong. Now she was all concern at the change from bright, outgoing businesswoman of a few hours earlier, to the wan-faced, silent woman who stood in front of her, all but wringing her hands with agitation. This was not a Claudia she had met before. 'Tell me, Claudia. What is it?'

'No—it's nothing. I'm being stupid. I——' She turned away, head hanging so that a black fall of hair concealed her face. Before Susie could take stock of the situation, Keith came sweeping in through the double doors with a broad smile over his face. Susie looked bewildered at the difference in their demeanours, and Keith's words only added to her confusion.

'Who's the flavour of the month, then?' he demanded with uncharacteristic verve. He shot a puzzled look in Susie's direction. 'Everything all right, Su?'

'You tell me, Keith. I'm completely in the dark. Have you got a contract, or haven't you?'

Checked momentarily, Keith shot a look of surprise at Claudia. 'Haven't you told her the good news yet?'

With a deep indrawn breath, Claudia faced them both. This was something she had to do, and there was no time like the present. 'I'm sorry, I know you've both been one hundred per cent behind this franchise idea, but despite the positive reception from Country House

Hotels, I'm afraid I can't really consider it seriously.'

'What?'

'But I don't understand——'

If Keith was shocked, Susie was confused. Feeling that she could only explain properly when she had managed to arrange her thoughts in better order, Claudia ran a hand over her forehead and, turning away towards the stairs, she added, 'Please don't discuss this with the rest of the staff yet. I'm going up to the flat to lie down. I—I've got a splitting headache,' she lied. 'I'll try and talk to you both later on.'

Without waiting to see how they took this offer, she turned on her heel and made her way up the carpeted stairs to the convenient little flat she had had fitted out on the top floor of the building. This was her sanctuary, her refuge when the demands of work were too pressing, and it was with a feeling of relief that she closed the door firmly behind her, kicked off her shoes and fixed herself an unaccustomed drink.

Though she had schooled herself over the years never to dwell on the past, now it seemed that a single breach in the dam threatened to bring the whole thing down on her. All the carefully tended defences were being swept away in an uncheckable flood of emotion.

Flinging herself down on the silk-covered divan by the window, she let the memories swamp her, hoping that in one kill or cure blast of recollection she could purge the agony of this unexpected confrontation with her past.

CHAPTER TWO

'SUSIE, come in, and bring Keith with you. I owe you both an explanation.'

Claudia tapped her pen on the grey marble inkwell, into which Susie daily and whimsically arranged an appropriate posy of flowers to match the décor, and waited for them to come up. There wasn't the vestige of an excuse in her head. What reason could she give for turning down the contract they'd all three been avid for only three hours earlier? Susie had already bounced into the office ahead of Keith before she had made up her mind what to tell them.

'Well?' she challenged swiftly, before Susie could open her mouth. 'I'm sorry if you both expected a contract to materialise out of this morning's preliminary meeting——' She stopped, correcting herself, 'exploratory meeting, I mean.' 'Preliminary' made it sound as if she might eventually be persuaded to say yes. 'I'm sure you realise, Keith,' she went on, craftily, she thought, enlisting his aid in her subterfuge, 'that Country House Hotels Ltd is, at this stage in their development, too new, not well enough established, to give us the security we need for a venture such as ours.'

'Not what?' Keith was moved to exclaim. 'But it's an old family firm, and Daniel Sinnington has acquired an impressive reputation since taking over——'

'Yes, but ideally we need a company that is already linked to our kind of business in some way. Plus, they've already admitted that they're in the process of opening up several new hotels in the next six months. It's obvious where their energies will be directed. I just feel we'll get a raw deal if we——'

'But they're exactly what we're after, surely? New dynamic managing director, full of energy and ideas. A group of new hotels will be an ideal place to start—no danger of upsetting the status quo, we'll be accepted from the start. Claudia, I don't understand. We've gone over all this——'

Keith's usual control had left him and the look of utter incomprehension on his face was given more expression by Susie bursting out, 'He's right, Claudia! It's crazy to back out if there's a chance, with Daniel Sinnington trailing clouds of glory wherever he goes.'

'What do you know about—about him?' stammered Claudia.

'Surely you read the local papers?'

'No, actually. I don't have time to do more than skim them now and then—I——'

'There was a profile of him not so long ago——'

'We won't go into that.' Claudia cut her off in mid-sentence. 'He's hardly relevant to the present issue.' The blatant lie brought an unexpected rush of colour to her cheeks, and she half turned away from them, as if keen to get on with something else. 'The way I see it, it's too big a risk——'

'But——'

'Sorry, Keith. You did a terrific job. But I can't help feeling that we would be taking on too much.' Again she tried to convey that she was eager to get on, and she looked at her watch as if to suggest that she had an imminent appointment, even though Susie wouldn't fall for that for a moment.

She felt as guilty as hell at having to cover up for herself, and Keith's bitter exclamation of disappointment as she closed the door on them both brought a twinge of remorse. He had worked hard on her behalf, even though she was by no means his only client, and now she had dashed his hopes. She knew he wanted to get rid of his free-lance work and take on the job of financial director for her full-time. She had wanted it too; indeed, it had been her idea in the first place. Now she had raised his hopes, only to bring them crashing down. She would be lucky if she managed to keep him at this rate. For all his solidity, he was ambitious—it was hardly his fault if he had been born middle-aged—and she couldn't expect him to dedicate himself to a business that seemed to be going nowhere. Susie too, when things had been hard, had always stood by her, turning down at least one offer to go over to one of the rivals that had mushroomed in a copycat attempt to cash in on her pioneering methods. What would Susie do if she thought they had reached a dead-end? Stop worrying, woman, she chided herself. They'll both get over it. Relax, will you?

For the first time since Daniel's silver gaze had trickled so arousingly over her body that morning, she forced herself to wind down. As the text books recommended, after the completion of an unpleasant task or a defeat, the thing to do is to go right on to the next job. Picking up her car-keys, she headed purposefully towards the door.

Braving Susie's deliberate glare as she went out, she made a conscious effort as she walked round the back to the car park to forget Claudia Gray for a few hours. She would square things with Susie and Keith as soon as an opportunity arose. After all, they could like it or lump it—she was the one who had to carry the can if anything went wrong. They would have to learn to trust her.

As she slid the car on to the High Street she knew she was fooling herself if she thought she was happy with the situation, but there was a softer smile on her face as she drove along. Toby would be waiting. Claudia Grey can go take a running jump, she told herself. There's more to life than work.

'He's rung three times already, and it's still not half-past nine,' Susie complained as soon as Claudia set foot in the salon next morning, after dropping Toby off. As she opened her mouth to ask who 'he' was, the phone shrieked again.

'Yes? She's here right now——' Susie held out the phone, but Claudia backed off, warning bells suddenly clanging.

'Who is it?' she mouthed.

'Daniel Sinnington, of course.' Susie gave her a searching look, and kept her hand clamped over the mouthpiece. 'I expect you'll come clean about all this one day, Claudia.' She gave her friend a forgiving smile. 'Would you rather take the call upstairs in your office?'

Claudia was already heading smartly for the door. 'I'd rather not take the call at all. Tell him I've had to go straight out again,' she called from out of the ruins of her shattered complacency.

'No way! I'm putting him through!' Susie called after her. There was the unmistakable sound in her voice of having got one over on Claudia. 'Putting you through now, Mr Sinnington,' she purred into the mouthpiece.

Claudia paused long enough to mouth one extremely rude word at her assistant before resigning herself to the inevitable. She made him wait though, taking off her coat and sitting down behind her desk before pressing the switch that would bring his voice honeying through her defences as if the previous night had never existed. Did I or did I not stay awake the whole night hyping myself up to stone-wall any attempt he might make to get me to sign a contract with him? she asked herself rhetorically.

'Good morning, lovely,' came the voice to wipe out

any such resolution.

'Who is this?' she demanded crisply.

'Come on, Claudia, do you always get into work so late?'

'Late? I'm not running a hotel. *I* don't have to breakfast my customers like you——' Too late, she realised she had given herself away.

'I hoped you'd recognise my voice.'

'Oh, very clever, Mr Sinnington——' she began.

Before she could go on, he was lowering his voice suggestively to ask, 'May I breakfast you some time, Mrs Gray?'

'Certainly not!'

'It wouldn't be the first time——' he murmured, with laughter in his voice.

'For goodness' sake, this is a public telephone! I mean—you know what I mean—your switchboard . . .' Embarrassed, she could only squirm as she heard the teasing laughter from the other end of the line.

'This is my private phone. Don't worry, I can be discreet, Mrs Gray. But seriously, what about breakfast? Lunch? Dinner?'

'All three?' she was jerked into asking.

'Why not?'

'Don't be ridiculous!' She took a deep breath. 'Look, we've thought over the contract very carefully at this end, and decided to say no. I'm afraid that's all I have to say——' She was about to drop the phone down on its hook, when she was stunned to hear it disconnect at the other end. At first she thought he must have accidentally disconnected himself, but when after ten minutes had passed and he still hadn't rung back, she began to assume that he had taken her rebuttal to heart and this was his way of showing his displeasure.

She told Susie as much when she came in with her list of appointments a few minutes later.

'Funny, I wouldn't have put him down as the petulant type,' Susie remarked, 'though, of course, I've only spoken to him on the phone.'

With effort, Claudia switched to the matter in hand.

'The new aerobics teacher seems to be getting some enthusiasm from her bunch,' she remarked.

'Yes, she's very keen. Good woman, that.'

'We ought to try to squeeze in an extra session some time. What about Friday lunch times?'

'Yoga.'

'It's a small group. Maybe they could move somewhere else?'

'Where? The cloakroom?'

'Perhaps another time would suit them? Aren't they mainly housewives? A morning session might fit the bill.'

'I'll mention it. You might be right. But look at this, Claudia,' Susie indicated the neatly typewritten sheet she had placed on the desk, 'I've weeded out the applicants for the vacancy for beautician and drawn up a short-list.'

Claudia scanned the list of names and the brief outline of the girls' previous experience.

'But of course,' Susie interrupted tartly, 'if there aren't going to be any new jobs, we may as well tear this up and let them all know they've been wasting their time.' Her clear green eyes were watching Claudia closely. Pinned, she shifted uncomfortably in her leather chair.

'Oh, Susie, trust me, do. I feel I'm doing the right thing. I do really.'

'Right for whom? The business—or yourself?'

'Myself, I suppose——' she admitted truthfully.

'I can't argue with you, then, Claudia. I guessed when I saw you yesterday after the meeting that something pretty cataclysmic had happened. But we've known each other for ages, and I thought we had no secrets from each other.' Susie was hurt, though she was trying not to show it, and it served to make Claudia feel even more uncomfortable. Was she right to sacrifice a major advance for them all, just because she couldn't cope with the situation?

'It's a very personal matter,' she defended herself. 'I'm sorry, love. I—I haven't quite come to terms with it myself yet.'

'When you do,' Susie's voice was warm, 'you know you can count on me. In the mean time,' she shrugged, 'I guess I'll just have to trust you, won't I? You've always delivered the goods before. Why not this time as well?' A look of concern crossed her face. 'I ought to warn you, though, Keith is feeling pretty sore at you. I think if you could just say something to calm him down, life will be a little sweeter for us all.'

She went out and Claudia felt that, on balance, Susie's stated loyalty made her feel worse than outright hostility would have done. If only she could have confided in her she knew it would have helped her to see things in a more balanced light. Perhaps she was making a mountain out of a molehill? Perhaps the danger she envisaged was simply a mixture of imagination and guilt? What had her life to do with the man, after all? She had no intention of dating him, let alone inviting him into her private life, and their relationship would be strictly business.

Apart from that, he obviously thought her trade name—Claudia Gray—was her name in marriage and, if nothing else, that assumption should keep him safely at arm's length. A sudden thought made her stomach turn to lead. It hadn't crossed her mind before, but perhaps he himself had married, in which case all these feverish speculations were pointless and he had no more intention of trying to pick up the relationship again than she had. Instead of feeling relieved, the thought left her with an unpleasant feeling of emptiness. At least it suggested to her that it might, after all, be safe to think again about the contract. Though there was still the possibility that her brief conversation with him over the phone just now had scotched their chances, anyway. How odd that he should simply disconnect like that . . .

Preoccupied, she donned a peach-coloured overall and went down into the salon to see how things were progressing.

'We're fully booked this morning, Mrs Gray,' Jill, one of the beauticians, emerged from between the peach cotton curtains that made the half-dozen cubicled areas of seclusion with a cheerful smile, obviously pleased to be busy.

'Good, that's nice to hear.' Claudia made to move on, but Jill detained her.

'I heard Susie was interviewing for another assistant yesterday,' she paused, a hand on the curtain before going back to continue her treatment.

'Yes, she interviewed several girls, but they aren't going to be working here.' Claudia bit her lip, not wishing to get into a discussion about future plans. Especially one that wasn't going to come off. But she knew, without the confirmation of eager curiosity written all over Jill's face, that the place was agog with rumour. 'We'll have to look into the possibility of creating a little more space in here, perhaps, then we can take on another pair of hands.'

'That would certainly ease things,' Jill gave a quick glance round the salon. 'Though where she would work, I can't imagine!'

Claudia exchanged a non-committal smile before the girl disappeared from sight. She had hit the nail on the head as far as Claudia was concerned. There was simply nowhere for them to expand. It was the second time she had been told as much in the space of half an hour. And it was this realisation that had prompted her to approach Country House Hotels in the first place. Now she was setting herself up to go through the whole business again—preliminary letters outlining the franchise idea, follow-ups to any queries, if, indeed, they managed to get a favourable response in the first place. She couldn't guess what part luck had played in getting them to the verge of signing a contract with Daniel's company. What if nobody else fell for the concept?

Her frown faded as a heady scent filled the air. Perfumed oil—a mixture of rose, ylang ylang and sandalwood, at a guess. Aromatherapy had been a successful innovation.

'That's lovely,' she murmured as she peeked in through the cubicle curtains to watch Annette massaging one of her regular clients' arms with the oil. Mrs Jessel—the Hon Mrs Jessel, to give her her full title, waved a heavily beringed finger at Claudia.

'Good morning, my dear. I'm going to swan out of here feeling like a million dollars again,' she called.

'That's what we aim for,' smiled Claudia. She got a real thrill when clients were so obviously delighted with their treatments. She knew from past conversations that, despite Mrs Jessel's undoubted good fortune in being so effortlessly wealthy, she had suffered recently from a series of family misfortunes that had made her a far from happy woman.

Claudia knew what it was like to be so low that life didn't seem worth living. There had been a time when her whole world seemed to have collapsed around her. Eighteen, unmarried and penniless, and trying to earn enough to keep body and soul together. A bad time.

Best to forget all that. She shook herself. The past seemed to be closing in on her right now—though it wasn't surprising in the circumstances, she supposed.

She wouldn't give in to it. Not now. She was a different person to the *ingénue* of yesteryear. Work was her never-failing cure-all these days.

Checking the appointments book took up a few minutes and, that task completed, she had just put the book back in its drawer when the light from reception blinked rapidly above the door.

It would be Susie, no doubt. She made her way back towards reception. Knowing that a more detailed explanation for her back-down over the contract was fast becoming overdue, she determined to try to put things straight at once.

'Susie—I——' The words hung unfinished in mid-air.

An incongruously masculine bulk loomed towards her from beside one of the potted palms. Tall, blond, breath-stopping, he could only make her goggle.

'You lead, I'll follow,' he greeted her tersely.

'I—I beg your pardon?' Stunned to see him materialise without warning, her confused brain could make no sense of his words.

'To your office, I mean—for starters, anyway,' he added, with a leer that would have done justice to the villain in a Victorian melodrama.

'You haven't got an appointment,' she pointed out, refusing to budge from the doorway. Her eyes flicked towards Susie's leather-bound day-book.

'It's all right. I've checked. You're free.'

'Th-thank you for telling me,' she managed to stutter. Her feebleness was appalling, she cursed herself. Shooting daggers at Susie, who was patently enjoying the spectacle of the cool Claudia Gray going weak at the knees and, by the look of it, weak in the head as well, she managed to stumble forward, then with an effort she pulled herself together.

'I'll deal with you later,' she snarled softly, as she led

the way past the desk to the stairs, and gave a very pointed glance at the open diary as she did so. 'While you're at it, you may as well do the job properly and chalk my schedule up on a blackboard outside.'

Susie's response was non-verbal—the expression in her dancing eyes merely question marks.

'You're obviously used to charming your way past receptionists, Mr Sinnington,' she remarked caustically, reading Susie's smitten expression aright. She ran two at a time up the narrow stairs to the office above, noting that he had no difficuilty in keeping up with her. When the door brought her to a momentary halt, his body, lightly grazing her own on the narrow landing, made her recoil from the blatant physicality of his touch as if stung.

'Nice intimate old building you've got here,' he murmured, grey eyes lazing over her hot and bothered expression with repressed amusement.

Without delaying long enough to answer, she pushed her way into the office and didn't feel safe again until she had managed to put the solid expanse of her desk between them.

CHAPTER THREE

'Do TAKE a seat,' invited Claudia coldly as Daniel prowled about the tiny room. It seemed to have shrunk like something out of *Alice*, and she felt like a very small creature trapped in a lion's cage. 'Do you make a habit of barging into places?' she attacked, in an attempt to remind them both that this was her territory, not his, and it was her right to call the shots.

'It depends whether the situation warrants it,' he replied imperturbably, 'and our telephone conversation suggests it did.' He came to rest in the quilted visitor's chair opposite. He looked so big she was afraid he would end up on the floor, and he noticed the involuntary smile as she pictured the scene.

'So it is some sort of game, is it? Catch-me-if-you-can?' He quirked an eyebrow. 'I guessed you couldn't be serious about turning down such an offer as ours. Especially as it was you who approached us in the first place.'

She drew back. 'I can assure you, Mr Sinnington, this is no game. I said no and I meant it. I don't,' she added, 'indulge in games at the expense of either my company's reputation or my employees' jobs.'

'That's what I would have thought,' he agreed. 'That's why I've been at a loss to explain this U-turn of yours.'

'It should surely be obvious why we can't consider working together?' she bit out.

His face softened in a rueful smile, making him look engagingly boyish and denying the air of executive

30

authority he wore. Claudia's fingers curled tightly at the end of her desk with the effort of controlling the rampaging of her emotions. He gave her a lingering look to ambush her intentions.

'Oh, Claudia, do you mean our adolescent love-affair? That's so sweet of you. But it can't surely be the only reason for such a drastic decision? Why, it happened all of twelve years ago——'

Thirteen, she corrected silently, staring tight-lipped at him. Teenage love-affair it might have been for him, but for her it had had repercussions, which he knew very well. Anger at the man's insensitivity churned up her thoughts again, making it impossible to reply.

Misinterpreting her silence, he hastened to enlarge on what he had said. 'I'm not belittling what you meant to me. And I won't deny I used to dream of meeting you again some time, some place, preferably with a full orchestra and sunset accompaniment, but we're both twelve years older now, we know life isn't like that.'

His repetition of the twelve-year gap he imagined between now and then was like a spark to an oil leak.

'At least get the year right,' she clipped, white-lipped with the strain of holding down her anger. 'It was thirteen years ago, actually.'

'Thirteen? OK. Twelve, thirteen—I'm flattered you remember, considering how it ended. I guess that surprises me.'

Her eyes dilated with shock. Did the man imagine she had no heart at all? So she had been called cold, frigid, but he surely didn't expect her to have forgotten that year, of all years, did he?

'You're a real joker, Danny, just like in the old days,' she managed to wheeze. It had been hell enough when he had ignored her letter, so painfully written, but to have simply erased the whole incident from his mind, the when and the what, opened up deep wounds that she had thought long since healed.

The pain at such callous indifference re-emerged, bringing a memory of those dreadful days when she had waited and waited for some reply from him. Anything, she'd felt then in her desperation, would have put things to rights—a word, a phone call, anything—just a sign that he was still there. But each day had been like the one before, a further nail hammered into her coffin.

Afterwards, she'd been forced to conclude that he had never cared. It was as simple and devastating as that.

Now it was pain to be reminded of that experience all over again. The look on his face was pure pantomime, she was sure, as he leaned towards her, bright eyes travelling caringly over her face.

'Claudia, we're both adult now, with all kinds of urgent responsibilities, and I know you'd be the last to let past mistakes dictate the present. Whatever happened or didn't happen then, let's wipe the slate clean. I'm sure you haven't got as far as this in the business world without being able to put personal matters on ice when necessary. All I want to say is, let's keep things simple. Get the contract agreed. And then let's see what happens next. At the moment, I don't think either of us can see the wood for the trees, with all these emotional issues clouding the scene.'

'Speak for yourself,' she murmured, half to herself. 'Things have never been clearer.' She paused, aware of what else he was saying. He was offering her the chance to climb down without loss of face, aware, no doubt, of how much she needed to take up the chance of a franchise with his company, and she was in agreement with what he said about the need to put personal issues on ice when the necessity arose. She would be foolish to turn him down. At the same time, she had a sneaking feeling that affairs of the heart, old pain and the waywardness of the emotions, were not so easily frozen into extinction as he seemed to think. Damn it, she'd tried for thirteen years, hadn't she? And look where it had got her—weak as a kitten at the mere sight of him!

It was a while before she was able to bring herself to speak. Daniel sat back, giving her all the time she needed, without pressuring.

'Is it possible?' she muttered, softly. 'Can the past be wiped out like that?' Seeing his look of bewilderment, she went on, 'Maybe you're right. I think I may have over-reacted on more than one occasion.' She gave a wry smile. 'It was a shock, bumping into you after so long, especially in a situation like that, when I was already keyed up.' Her rational side began to wake up, persuading her to his view. 'After all,' she continued more briskly, 'no doubt we've both been in love a hundred times since that summer. Life couldn't go on if love always interfered with one's business dealings, could it?' Her eyes narrowed in the gleam of a smile, though there was little humour in it. 'Don't you agree, Daniel?'

He shot her an odd look. 'I'm not sure about your assumptions there——' He seemed to flounder, his quicksilver glance aimed at penetrating her façade of swiftly assumed nonchalance.

His confusion pleased her. 'If you can let me see the draft contract as soon as possible, I don't see why we can't get things moving quite soon. As you say, it all happpened long ago and we're both now fully committed to our *adult* responsibilities.' She gave a brittle laugh. 'I've already told you I never mix business with pleasure. It's just that you gave the impression that that's what you wanted.' It was satisfying to see his eyes turn battleship-grey.

'Claudia, let's leave it for the time being, shall we?' he clipped. 'If we talk now, we'll only add to our misunderstandings.'

'Suits me.' She rose to her feet, effectively concluding their meeting. 'Would you like me to see you out or can you find your own way?'

'I expect I'll manage.'

'I'm sure you will,' she breathed with an enigmatic smile.

It took only two strides for him to cross the tiny room, and at the door he paused with his hand on the latch. 'Why is it,' he asked measuringly, 'you seem to have got the upper hand?'

When he left, without waiting for a reply, she buzzed Susie to tell her to show him out. It would have been easy to answer his question—she had survived thirteen years of putting her feelings on ice. She had been in control for all but the first of them, and she wasn't about to let her advantage slip now.

Emotions neatly packaged once again, she went down to have a word with Susie when she was sure he had left the building.

'What did he do, twist your arm?' she asked brightly, when Claudia told her the deal was on again.

'You're joking! I wouldn't let a playboy like that within touching distance of my arms,' she replied coolly.

'So you did read the profile in the Press, after all,' Susie smiled.

'No. What do you mean?'

Rummaging in her desk drawer, Susie pulled out a dog-eared magazine. She flicked through until she came to the page she wanted, then she read, '"With the exception of eldest son, Daniel, they are an ascetic, antisocial family, applying themselves to the serious business of adding to their already considerable fortune.

Only Daniel has an appetite for expensive pleasures, which makes his inheritance advantageous. Irresistibly attractive, with a sweet charm, he has had countless girlfriends".' She stopped. 'There, nothing about whether he's married or not. But I pity his wife if he is.'

'Honestly, Susie, how can you take any notice of the trash they write in gossip columns?' replied Claudia virtuously. 'And his private life has absolutely nothing to do with us. I'd prefer it if we could have a chat about job definition, perhaps?'

Susie stopped smiling. 'What do you mean?'

'It's obvious, isn't it? You just let that man in here without any warning—it could have been difficult——'

'It worked out all right, didn't it?'

Claudia was surprised to see Susie flush hotly and, to her further astonishment, she saw her get up and go over to the filing cabinet, as if bent on a sudden task of some urgency. Nonplussed, Claudia waited for her to say something, but when she didn't she felt compelled to add, 'By the way, what about letting Keith know the good news, if he's been so worried? I don't mind if you claim I've made a U-turn . . .' She smiled. 'I can always deny it later.'

To her relief, Susie returned her smile this time. 'Will do. You're going to make him a very happy man.'

The draft contract came in by messenger later that morning, just as Keith called by to hear the good news in person. Together, the three of them looked it over, pleased to see that it conformed to the letter with the matters they had discussed the previous day.

'Let's get this over to our solicitors right away,' Claudia suggested.

'Yes. I'll take it,' offered Susie.

'Then we'll—er—get the show on the tracks?' offered
Keith jauntily.

'Road, Keith, it's "show on the road"—but never
mind, Claudia and I know what you mean.'

We do indeed, thought Claudia to herself, sliding the
stiffly folded documents back inside their buff envelope.

A few days later, the pop of champagne corks ushered in
a new era for the salon, in which all the staff
participated, for by this time the changes ahead had been
detailed to every employee, full and part-time. It meant
that it was quite a gathering in the exercise studio, and
Claudia watched the ink dry on the contract where she
had signed above Daniel's name with mixed feelings. It
felt like more than just a business contract, for it was as if
something from long ago, which was not yet finished,
had been brought back to life.

As the celebrations began to draw to a close, she
wended her way with a vague smile through the maze of
abandoned champagne glasses, just as the phone in
reception shrilled out, bringing her hazily back into the
present. She managed to reach it before anyone else had
woken up to the fact that it was ringing, but when she
heard the familiar voice she nearly wished she hadn't.

'Hello, lovely, signed the contract yet?'

'All done——' she began, but he interrupted before
she could finish.

'Good,' he said, 'then it's OK to invite you to dinner?
I'll pick you up at the salon in twenty minutes.'

'Hey, wait a minute!'

He had obviously been about to put the phone down,
because his voice came from farther away. 'What's the
matter?' he asked smoothly, coming closer to the
mouthpiece. 'You haven't already eaten, have you?'

'No, but——' she stopped wishing she could bite off her tongue. 'That's not the point, Daniel. Who said anything about dinner? You're making a big assumption if you think——'

'Listen. Tell me all about it in twenty minutes. No, make it fifteen. And don't drink any more champagne till I get there.'

The line went dead.

'Well, of all the——' She looked suspiciously at the receiver, as if expecting it to flare into life again, but it simply burred back at her like a contented cat. 'Oh, well,' she thought aloud philosophically, 'if he wants to waste his time coming over here, tough on him!'

'Tough on who, darling?' Susie tottered into view with one arm comfortably around Keith's shoulders.

'Daniel Sinnington, who else?' she muttered, vaguely disconcerted to see her normally staid accountant with his tie metaphorically hanging loose.

Susie looked suddenly guilty and started to gather up the empty glasses, without actually relinquishing her hold on Keith's supporting arm. When the job was done, Claudia was forced to ask the question that had been gnawing at her.

'Susie,' she began, 'am I merely paranoid, or do you really look shifty every time Daniel's name is mentioned?'

'I'm the genuine article, Claudia—your one and only shifty secretary!' She began to giggle.

'I fail to see the joke,' Claudia replied huffily. 'Firstly there's nothing amusing in your peculiar behaviour, and there's certainly nothing funny about having Daniel Sinnington breathing down my neck at every turn. The man must be psychic—it's quite unnerving. How on earth did he know we were here late tonight? Does he think I live and breathe work?' The idea was faintly unattractive.

Susie giggled again. 'He may not be psychic without a hotline to my day-book, but he sure has hypnotic eyes—hey, Keith baby, shut your ears to all this. It's girl talk.'

'I'll run her home,' he muttered anxiously to Claudia.

'Run her over, for all I care,' replied Claudia. She turned to the giggling blonde. 'Susie, do you mean you've been leaking news of my activities to that—*man*?'

'I'm just a girl who can't say no,' she lisped.

'Come on, old girl, you've put away too much champagne for one evening——'

'Yes. Take her out of my sight, Keith, before I do something I'll regret, and get her safely home before anybody else gets the same idea!'

A sound at the street door made her spin. 'Why, hi, Daniel,' she breezed falsely. 'We were all just leaving. Nice of you to call. Pity you've missed the party.' And before he could draw breath she added, 'Shame I can't have dinner with you tonight.'

'We'll be getting along, Claudia.' Keith dragged Susie out with him, though not before she had shamelessly dimpled a welcome at Daniel.

When they had gone he remained draped in the doorway, his eyes a smouldering silver as they burned over her. 'You know,' he began conversationally, 'I always feel as if I'm getting the worst of the deal whenever I come in here. Besides which,' he started to walk slowly towards her, 'it's like a doll's house. I'm afraid to assert myself in case I smash the furniture.' He moved lazily within reach, all the lithe grace of him abruptly wiping any rational thought from her mind. She gaped, as if mesmerised, at the muscular attraction of him in his impeccable white shirt and dinner-jacket.

'You look as if you've been celebrating something,'

she muttered, vaguely put out at the thought that he had come on from somewhere else.

'Not yet,' he replied succinctly. 'But I aim to.'

Before she could stop him, he had lifted her right hand and placed his lips gently on the back of it. The warmth from his fingers seemed to melt her resistance and she felt powerless to move away. Her momentary immobility gave him the chance to trail his lips provocatively over the back of her hand to the inside of her wrist, only coming to rest with a slight increase of pressure inside her palm.

'Don't do that,' she protested huskily, unable to snatch her hand away.

'Why not? You like. I like. Why not?'

'No!'

His hold increased measurably to match the force she needed to break his grasp. Realising how undignified a skirmish would look, she left her hand in his, deliberately cutting off her sensations so that it lay like a lump of dead meat between his fingers.

'I thought you said that personal matters were to be put on ice?' she accused. 'Surely that excludes dinner dates?'

'I said no such thing,' he argued, her hand still lying limply in his own. 'What I actually said was that both of us are able to put personal matters on ice when necessary.'

'It amounts to the same thing,' she mocked. We are, true, and it *is* necessary. Now, let me go.'

He ignored her request, and instead narrowed his eyes as if working something out. 'Seems there's a serious difference of opinion here, Claudia,' he informed her humorously. 'If you remember what else I said—which obviously you don't—I suggested we kept things simple until after the contract was signed.'

Her eyes darkened as she realised what he was getting at. 'Hence your question over the phone?'

'And your answer was, I believe, "all done", so——'

'Oh, you!' she snarled, furiously refusing to recognise the humorous tilt to his lips. 'You think you're so clever. Well, you're not in a court of law now, so you can take your insufferable penchant for pedantry elsewhere!'

She hadn't meant to sound funny, and her furious expression, as such a quaint phrase fell from her lips, made him chuckle softly, adding to her fury.

'If you imagine I'm going to let you get away a second time, dear Claudia, you'll have to think again.'

'W-what do you mean, Daniel?'

'I mean, to hell with Mr Gray, wherever he is, and this——' He pulled her forward and brought his blond head unbearably close. As he still had a firm hold of her wrists, she was powerless to step out of range and watched fascinated, for an age it seemed, while his smiling lips hovered just above her own.

'No!' she managed to croak, just before they came down to claim her own in a kiss of ineffable sweetness. For a moment she responded blindly, hungrily, until warning bells alerted her to the slippery path ahead if she succumbed to his philandering. He noticed at once the sudden hardening of her mouth and the way her body stiffened unresponsively in his arms, and it made him draw back with a puzzled smile.

'More games, Claudia?'

'No games. Leave me alone,' she muttered, stumbling against him in an effort to free herself.

'If I thought you really meant it I would,' he informed her coolly.

'Oh, I see.' She raised her head and her lip curled. 'You're one of these macho men who think no means yes. Well, let me tell you, Mr Daniel Sinnington, in my book, no means——' But before she could finish, his hard male body matched her own length for length as his lips claimed hers again in pulsing ecstasy. Impossible to resist, he assailed her long pent-up store of naked desire, and feelings she had thought well damned up sprang instantly into renewed life. She tried to stifle her own feverish whispers of desire, which were like the pleas of some other woman, while he bestowed on long un-touched places the intimacy of his caress.

'No,' she whispered as his kisses became more intimate, her fingers unlacing from out of the bright strands of his hair. 'Someone may come in——' She tried to scrabble her blouse back inside the waistband of her skirt.

'People are still here?' he muttered. 'I thought everyone had left.' With a reluctant groan he gradually released her, only to keep pulling her back to bestow lingering little kises all over her face and neck.

'Please, Daniel, stop it! I'm supposed to be in charge here!'

'You're in charge of me, Claudia, isn't that enough? I still love you, you know. I never forgot.'

His words sent her back a pace out of his arms, bringing to the fore the anger she felt but which she had never been able to express. Keeping her distance, she straightened her clothes and gazed coldly across at him, drawing herself up as she spoke. 'You still find it too easy to say, don't you, Daniel?' Her lips tightened. 'It may have escaped your notice but I'm no longer a seventeen-year-old *ingénue*. I may have fallen for your charming ability to lie once, but I should warn you that it will never happen again, not if the oceans freeze over.'

With an effort she steadied her shaking hands and jammed them inside her jacket pockets. 'I'd prefer if we carried on as we agreed a few days ago. Keeping things simple. Right?'

'But, Claudia, that's not what you really want. And,' added Daniel more harshly, 'I do not lie, charmingly or otherwise.' He made as if to take her in his arms again, but she evaded them and drew back with an angry, rapid, brushing movement, as if annoyed by the attentions of a particularly nasty insect.

'It's a lie to say you love me,' she clipped. 'It was a lie then and it's a lie now. I'm not so naïve that I don't realise people say things in each other's arms that in calmer moments they know they don't mean.' She hesitated, the mere presence of him still weaving the old magic on her senses. 'But in the old days, I didn't know this. I guess I was a gullible little fool,' she added brusquely. 'Things are different now. I've changed.'

'But I was crazy about you.' He looked astonished. 'I loved you as seriously as an immature young lad can love——'

Her scornful laugh cut across his words. 'Do you seriously expect me to forget what the result of our so-called love was?' For a moment she hated him for trying to pull the wool over her eyes yet again, and it showed in her eyes, for his expression changed, darkening in response. He was about to speak when a group came out of the studio. It afforded Claudia the chance to pull herself together.

Looked at clearly, it was a straightforward situation, she told herself, forcing the complications back into the dark corner where they belonged.

Here was a handsome man, undeniably attracted to her and, as would be expected, hoping for a little 'adult love' to spice up the business routine. And here, too, was Claudia Gray, twenty-nine years old, displaying all the naïveté of a seventeen-year-old and taking his blatant flirting as seriously as ever! The trouble was, with any other man she could have played a sophisticated game with no danger of getting her fingers burned, but with Daniel it was different. It would always be different. He was the man she had loved all her adult life. It was her simple misfortune to be a once-in-a-lifetime type, and her double misfortune that the recipient of her fidelity should be a light-hearted flirt—humorous, generous, sexy and warm—but a flirt, a man for whom admiration had always been there for the asking, demanding nothing of him, no commitment, no loyalty—no constancy.

There was one obvious way out—she could forget her anger with him. It was stale now, futile to blame a fully grown man for the mistakes of his boyhood. And instead she could try to teach herself his game, learn to play with a lighter touch. It was either that—or never set eyes on him again. She shuddered away from that alternative. The other was far better—and, God knew, there had been little fun in her life so far. Why shouldn't she enjoy his flattering attentions while they lasted?'

Stragglers from the studio eddied round them both, largely ignoring them as they piled up the empty glasses and generally set the place to rights, and she took the opportunity to come to stand beside him. 'Make me a promise, Daniel,' she demanded. 'Never talk to me of love.'

He gave her a strange look. 'And if I promise?'

'I'll have dinner with you!'

'More than once?'

'If you like.'

A grin broadened his features. 'How can I refuse an offer like that? Done!'

For security reasons they were the last to leave and, after they had gone round making sure everything was locked up properly, he took her by the hand and led her to his car, parked crazily half on the pavement and half off. There was no ticket on it.

'You're a lucky man, Daniel Sinnington,' she remarked, as she waited to climb in.

'I know,' he told her with a lop-sided smile. 'I'm counting on it.'

Perhaps because he had caught her new mood and intuitively realised that some unwritten contract had been agreed between them, he didn't drive to the small, exclusive restaurant in the country, where he had already booked a candle-lit table for two, but instead took her to the newest, brashest wine bar in town. With its noisy rabble of trend-setting younger folk, and its laser show and continuous hit chart sounds, it was impossible to talk, and she thought he guessed how relieved she was by this. It was also impossible to dance on such a crowded floor, so instead they sat close together, establishing a new unspoken intimacy that was easy going and friendly. When he dropped her off at her flat above the salon a little after midnight, she thanked him quickly and climbed out of the car before he could detain her. By the time she had climbed up to her room, the street below the window was empty except for the on-off flashing of a shop sign further down. She felt strangely desolate. A pattern for the future? she asked herself as she drifted swiftly sleepwards. And I promised myself I wouldn't date him . . . well, I shan't, except for fun times like tonight. We'll keep it light—and uncommitted—and casual . . . and then everything will be all right.

CHAPTER FOUR

EVERY time the phone bleeped beside her on the desk, Claudia jumped. It had been nearly a week now, and Daniel had failed to follow up their previous date with any further invitations. So much for imagining she had the whip-hand and could choose whether he was kept safely at a distance or not! She was angry with herself for so easily falling for him all over again as well, for it was all very well pretending that she had her feelings neatly packed away in an ice-box, but all it took was three or four days of silence to have her grabbing for the phone like a lovesick teenager. Firmly she repeated to herself that it was best this way. And then jumped when the phone bleeped again, and her heart leaped heedlessly into her mouth once more.

'Yes, Susie?' she snarled, recognising the voice.

'Don't sound like that. I haven't done it yet,' came the reply from the other end. Then, more seriously she went on, 'I wondered if you'd remembered that Jill was having the day off?'

'Yes, and Sharon can't cover for her because her seven-year-old is off school with summer flu——' And at once they were into the thick of the day and it was going to be as hectic as usual. When she replaced the receiver and paused before tackling the next task, she wondered why her days were so full and her evenings so empty. At least she had a supper date with some friends who lived out of town. She would probably wind up spending the night at Lake House. When Toby wasn't around she rarely used the house in the country, finding it more convenient to stay in the flat above the salon. The vastness of Lake House underlined the loneliness of having only one person in it.

Half-way through the morning, when Claudia was in the middle of a facial, Susie's voice broke through her thoughts over the intercom in reception. 'Phone call, Claudia. Personal.'

Unable to leave her client, she asked Susie to take it. A few minutes later Susie's voice came through again. 'It was Mr Sinnington's secretary. She said would you call him when you're free.'

Would *I* call *him*? When he's taken a week to get back to me? she thought furiously. Not likely!

She maintained a resolute silence for the rest of the day but, by the time her escort, an old friend of a decidedly confirmed bachelor status, arrived to take her out to supper, it was clear that Daniel had no intention of trying to contact her again that day. So be it, she thought fatalistically. His lack of follow-up was a fitting comment on the importance he ascribed their relationship.

Peter had parked his car safely round the back of the building, the car park emptying fast at this time in the evening, and Claudia allowed him to tuck her into the fawn suedette passenger seat before he settled in beside her. She leaned her head back on the rest and closed her eyes. There was a lulling light orchestral piece on the stereo cassette, its soporific effect anything but what she wanted after a day of rush and bustle at work. She made a rapid calculation.

'I've been standing on my feet for three hours and twenty-five minutes without a break,' she told him, adding flippantly, 'I hope this is a sit-down supper and not a running buffet!'

'Oh dear, don't you feel up to it? If it's going to be too much for you we can go home and you can put your feet up instead——' His pleasant face showed total concern.

Instead of accepting it for what it was, Claudia felt an inexplicable rush of irritation. 'Oh for goodness' sake, stop being such an old maid, Peter! It was a joke. I'm twenty-nine, not ninety-nine!'

The look of bewildered hurt on his face made her feel guilty, it wasn't *his* fault she was in a mood, but she couldn't bring herself to apologise.

He slipped the brake off and started to edge cautiously towards the exit without saying anything, only to pull up with a jerk just as he'd begun to filter into the main road.

'Silly fool,' he muttered under his breath.

A familiar silver convertible was straddled across the pavement, its rear bumper dangerously close to the exit, not exactly blocking it, but causing Peter to stop, put his gears into reverse and try to make a tighter corner to clear it on his way out.

Claudia snapped her eyes open, then froze. Even as she noted the car causing the trouble she caught sight of its owner, all six-foot-plus of him striding purposefully out of the salon. Before she could shrink back in the vain hope that he wouldn't notice her, his attention was caught by the grinding and crashing of Peter's gear-box and his glance swept imperiously over the car and its occupants. He noticed Claudia at once. Without faltering, he headed straight for her. A peremptory fist rapped on the window.

'Who the dickens?' exclaimed Peter. Then, noticing Claudia's expression he asked, 'Friend of yours, Clau-

dia?' He was red-faced now, wrenching inexpertly at
the hand-brake.

'No—not a friend exactly,' she faltered, wanting
nothing to do with the man outside. Trouble was what
his whole demeanour spelled out, and she had no wish to
discover the reason why.

'Looks as if he's got something pretty important to
say.' Peter underlined the impression Daniel was
creating. 'Better open the window and see what it is.'

'Drive on, can't you? Aren't we late or something?'
she demanded, shrinking further back as Daniel rapped
once more on the window. With a whirr, the electrics
removed the only protection that lay between her and
the sparking wrath of the man outside. Then Daniel was
peering sardonicaly into the car, giving a brief examin-
ing glance towards Claudia's companion, before turning
to her with a smile from which all anger had been wiped
in an instant. His voice when it came, simply oozed a
kind of syrupy politeness. Claudia was not fooled for an
instant.

'Good evening, Mrs Gray. Obviously you didn't
receive my telephone message from your receptionist
this morning.'

'But yes, I did——' she began.

'I see . . .' He paused significantly and gave a small
shrug of his powerful shoulders, nonchalantly resting
one hand on the bottom edge of the window. She
scowled up at him, but before she could say anything he
went on smoothly, 'I rather hoped we could have had a
meeting before the day was out——'

'As you can see, I have an engagement this evening,'
she pointed out, with a level of hauteur in her tones that
was not lost on Daniel.

'Don't worry,' he replied smoothly, 'we'll simply

have to make our decisions without you.'

His smile, condescending in the extreme, prompted her to croak, 'What decisions? What about?'

'Don't worry your head about it,' he replied in such a patronising tone she wanted to scream. 'I'm sure you'll love the—er—the yellow and lime-green décor we've chosen for you.'

'The *what*?' She nearly leaped from the car.

He drew his lips back in a crocodile grin and turned lazily back towards the car. 'Better not block you in any longer. *Ciao*!'

His gesture of farewell was pure theatre. *Daniel Sinnington*, she seethed inwardly. Then, raising her voice, she shouted, 'Wait! Daniel!'

When he took no notice she scrabbled helplessly at the locked door, failing in her haste to find the catch. Yellow and lime green? He had to be joking!

'Open this damned door for me, Peter! Come on, hurry!'

Daniel was already folding his long length elegantly into the confines of his silver automobile, and obviously had no intention of responding to her call.

'Hurry, will you?' she almost shrieked at Peter. He, poor man, was shocked to the core to discover that his usually tranquil Claudia had been hiding a termagant beneath her cool façade. Now he dithered helplessly, while Claudia shouted Daniel's name once more, loud enough to startle someone on the opposite side of the street, but to her utter chagrin Daniel merely waved one hand in a casual sort of fashion and put his foot on the accelerator. She caught a glimpse of white teeth in the driving mirror as he bestowed a diminishing smile on her before throwing the car recklessly into midstream.

'Jolly good acceleration on those things,' observed

Peter as it became a blur up the road.

'Oh, shut up, do!' For the second time that evening Claudia felt she ought to apologise at once to poor Peter, and for the second time she deliberately failed to do so. This time Peter merely shrugged before edging out into the high street, following at a more sedate pace the track Daniel had recently blazed.

'Quite an impressive-looking chap,' Peter observed as they drove along. 'Who is he?'

'He's the one who's buying the franchise of my business,' she told him, irritated to have Daniel's obvious virility endorsed in this way by her escort for the evening. Almost bouncing with rage she added, 'He's a tricky devil and now he's obviously trying to put one over on me. Did you hear him? *Yellow and lime green*! If he thinks I'm going to run a chain of salons done out in colours like that, he must be mad! People would stay away in droves. *Nobody* could be so stupid as to think a colour scheme like that would work for our sort of image.'

Then she began to see the funny side. It wasn't something she could admit to Peter, but it was obvious what Daniel's game was—he was trying to rattle her as a punishment for not returning his call. It must be a unique experience to have a woman fail to respond to the Sinnington brand of charm. She gritted her teeth. In the morning she would ring him, apologise sweetly—then make sure she never got herself in this predicament again, by telling him plainly that there could be nothing between them. It proved one thing—she had been right to be wary. Despite his promises, he obviously had no intention of keeping their relationship on a platonic footing as he had tried to imply.

*　*　*

The evening with Peter's friends was mind-wreckingly dull—not their fault but Daniel's because his blazing silver eyes, turning from pure anger to hypocritical sympathy, would superimpose themselves continually over the scene before her, rendering it lifeless by comparison.

It was with relief that she afterwards sought out the solitude of Lake House and spent a restless night there, before setting off early next morning in order to avoid the rush-hour traffic streaming back into town.

The car park was still almost empty as she slid the car into its familiar place but an irate voice jolted her out of her preoccupation even before she had time to switch off the ignition.

'Where the hell did you get to last night? Don't tell me you spent a night on the tiles with that L-driver I saw you with after work!'

Claudia blinked at the irate face peering into her own.

'You didn't come back home, because I rang you and when there was no answer I called round. I rang the bell long enough to waken the dead. And who the hell *was* that, anyway? No, don't tell me it was your old man. That guy's name is Symes, not Gray. I suppose your husband, poor devil, is away on business. While the cat's away the mice will play, is that it?' His lip curled as he lowered his blond head to glare down at her where she still sat, as if stupefied, at the wheel of her two-seater sports car.

A restless night had left her feeling half-asleep this morning, and she felt too vulnerable to be confronted by Daniel, of all people, looming from behind a parked car before she was properly awake. He had appeared without any warning, wide awake, virile and with something menacing about him that brought waves of panic shivering through the veil of tiredness blurring her mind. Stifling a small yawn, she could only gaze at him as if he was the apparition that had haunted her half-sleep all through the night.

When he shot out a large hand and gripped hers as if to pull her bodily from the car, she knew at once that he was no apparition. A pulse of desire slammed through her body.

'Take your hands off me,' she managed to croak.

'What's sauce for the goose is—you know the rest,' he rasped back.

'What on earth are you talking about?' she demanded, striving to keep an even note in her voice.

His face was black with some emotion that boded no good for the recipient of his attentions. 'Did you think you could keep me in the dark?' he ground out. 'I'm not a complete fool, though God knows,' he added in an almost inaudible mutter, 'I could be a fool for you——' He broke off and gave her a black stare that made a tremble shake her body, and when she tried to speak she found her throat quite dry. Had the very thing she feared most now happened? Somehow or other, had he managed to find out about Toby? It seemed impossible, but there was no other explanation for this towering rage. Slithering beneath his grasp so that she was standing upright beside him, she turned on him, fear transforming itself into blind rage in an instant.

'Leave him alone, Daniel Sinnington. We want nothing to do with you. Do you hear? You're to keep away——' She felt cold all over and had to lean back against the tiny car, gaining some strength from the solidity of it pressing into the small of her back. As he loomed nearer she tried to push him away with both hands, but her attempt was futile, as if there was no strength left in her. His sheer closeness made her knees tremble so that she had to claw back the desire to cling to him, to yield to him whatever the consequences. It was a brief and bitter battle, the strain of it showing plainly in her eyes.

'Claudia——' His voice was roughened with emotion. 'I don't want to fight you—and I don't care what you get up to behind your husband's back. Live as you must. But please don't look like that—it's as if you're frightened of me.' His hand slid gently down the side of her face. 'I would never hurt you, Claudia. How could you think that?'

She wanted to cry out wildly that he was the only man who could, but his lips were only inches from her own and moving closer, paralysing her will. The fact that they were standing in a public car park at one of its busiest times, and ill-concealed by the low roof of the sports car against which she was being pressed, seemed of no importance to either of them. Relentlessly his lips came closer, and the hands which had reached out to crush her own in anger slithered like liquid heat over her slim form, splaying over her hips to drag them against his own with a sudden convulsive passion. Mercilessly he brought his mouth hotly down on to her own, blazing kisses over her sleepy skin, bringing it to pulsing life beneath the onslaught of his tender caress. She felt a groan of surrender rise to her throat. Impossible not to respond to him, whatever he believed about her, whatever he had discovered, and whatever retribution the truth would bring him to wreak on her. All that mattered at this one moment was the loving touch of the man for whom her body yearned.

Expertly teasing open her lips with the tip of his tongue, he drew on the well of her desire and she allowed her mouth to slacken, surrendering all common sense to him as she had done long ago, and moaning with pure happiness as his forgotten, once familiar touch awakened memories that had seemed to bring only pain. Her hair, pinned neatly to one side by a silver clip, slithered free as his fingers ranged through the silky strands. He clasped her heated face between both hands and brought her mouth up again and again to the plunging exploration of his tongue.

'You can't deny that something still exists between us, Claudia,' he murmured at last, against the side of her face. 'Let's go somewhere less public. We must talk this out——'

Claudia was not sure how long the sound of arriving cars had been going on, but when she cast a bleared glance over his shoulder she was horrified to see how public a place it really was. But Daniel's suggestion filled her with an even greater horror. What would he decide to do to her now he knew the truth? Trembling, she could only lean against him, as if her eventual persecutor would at the same time become her saviour.

'I'm sorry, Daniel. I'm so sorry for—I didn't mean to—I—I—never guessed we would ever meet again. There seemed no other way out. I——' She looked dazedly at him, her eyes meeting his openly and honestly. 'I didn't know how else to survive ... and knowing you didn't care a damn ...'

He pulled her head on to his shoulder and held it there, stroking the sleek dark hair over and over, comforting and vibrant with desire, too.

'You're not making much sense at the moment, but if you think I don't care you couldn't be further from the truth.' He gave a small laugh. 'You made me promise never to talk to you of love, so I won't. Let's just go inside and cool off.' He held her at arm's length. 'I hope the coast is clear, or is that why you spent the night elsewhere with your lover? Because your husband's back?'

There was an edge to his voice, and his lips curled as her eyes widened in astonishment.

'Could you feel anything for me if you really thought I'd just spent the night with a lover while my husband was waiting at home for me?' she asked, scandalised. 'It'd be so underhand!'

His smile was pure joy. 'I have a theory about you,' he replied. 'It makes you come out of this whole complicated mess as pure as Snow White. How about breakfast while I expound it to you? Then, when I'm feeling nice and safe, you can hit me with the horrible truth?'

Now totally confused by him, Claudia followed him across the car park, then let them both inside the building through the side door and, without encountering anyone, for it was still a good half-hour before anybody was due in, she led the way up the narrow staircase to the flat on the top floor.

While she brewed coffee and toasted a couple of muffins under the grill, he roamed around, getting in the way rather until she ordered him to go and open the windows in the next room. It was going to be a hot day, and the east-facing sitting-room was already stuffy.

'Here we are—breakfast,' she announced a few minutes later, setting the tray down and noting at the same time how the breeze from the open window ruffled his blond hair as he lolled on the chintzy two-seater sofa in the alcove. Then she nearly let out a cry, for he was holding a photograph of Toby in his hands, and staring at it intently, as if trying to make something out. As she opened her mouth to say something, he propped it back on the bookshelf and leaned forward to help clear a space for the tray. She tensed, expecting some comment, but he appeared to have forgotten the photograph instantly.

'Carry on, then,' she demanded bravely, as soon as they were both seated. 'Let's get it all over with.' She tried to make light of things in what seemed like the worst moment of her life—the only thing that gave her the courage to go on was his undoubted feeling for her. For the time being at least, these seemed to be warding off the worst of his wrath.

'My theory,' he announced, 'for what it's worth, is this. It seems obvious, especially having had a quick look round here, that you now live alone. I mean—there isn't room to swing a cat in here—your mythical Mr Gray would have to be a garden gnome. Claudia, I'm right, yes?'

She nodded. 'But why call him mythical?'

He smiled briefly. 'You tell me.'

She shook her head.

'Could it be that Mr Gray, bless his soul, no longer plays any part in your life?' His voice had softened, as if he was afraid of treading on dangerous ground. 'Am I right, Claudia? You're not together any longer, are you?' His grey eyes brushed over her, seeming more liquid, softer, not hurtful and sharp as before when he had been angry with her.

She was acutely aware of the irony of the situation. If she understood him properly he imagined she had been abandoned by her husband, hurt by him . . . Now she was on the horns of a dilemma, for how could she honestly deny a break-up with a man who had never existed? She avoided the problem, only managing to whisper, 'Go on. That's not all, is it? I don't call that a theory.'

'OK. Forget the word theory—shot in the dark would be more accurate—or a grasping at straws, perhaps?'

Her face burned when she caught his glance, as his expression confirmed the import of his words.

'Claudia. Answer me one way or the other, please? I'm not trying to pry, if it's still a painful memory for you——'

She shook her head quickly. It was painful, but not for the reasons he assumed. 'It's all right. There is no Mr Gray. I'm sorry if I deliberately led you to believe——' She hesitated. 'Sometimes it's easier like that, isn't it?'

He reached across the glass-topped table that divided them, and grasped her hand. 'I hate to think of anyone making you suffer, my love. I could throttle the man who——'

'No! Please, don't say that!' Guilt at allowing the misunderstanding to persist in any form made her express herself carelessly, and she could see that Daniel had misunderstood her once again—he thought she was defending an ex-husband, that she was still, perhaps, in love with him. The abandoned, ever-loving wife. Perhaps, after all, it wasn't so far from the truth.

'It's not what you think——' she began again, determined to clear things up as far as she could, without giving too much away. But before she could continue he pressed two fingers to her lips.

'I didn't intend this to be an inquisition. I'm sorry if I've been clumsy. I've no intention of prying—it's just that there's such an air of sadness about you—and something so chaste ... It makes me wonder why.'

Inexplicably, Claudia felt her eyes fill with tears. There was so much warmth in his voice, and it was what she had always dreamed of, yet it was coming too late and in the wrong context, so that she didn't know how to handle it. There was so much she wanted to tell him, about the years she had struggled on alone without ever having had the love and support of anyone, let alone a husband, that his unexpected concern seemed to undermine the self-reliance she had forced herself to develop. Ironically, she felt that now, when most of the danger was over, she was beginning to break.

Abruptly springing to her feet, she anounced with false brightness, 'I forgot the cream! Some hostess. You'll think twice about breakfasting with me in future, Daniel Sinnington!' She went to forage in the galley kitchen for cream she didn't even know she possessed, while prattling on in the same vein. Lighting on a frozen block of cream in a corner of the freezer, she ran the plastic pack noisily under the hot-water tap for a minute or two, calling through to him as she did so to start in on the muffins before they got cold.

'Would you like honey?' She appeared briefly in the doorway, dripping water and defrosted cream.

'Come here, you idiot. I only want you,' he growled.

'No, Danny.' She slipped back into the old name. It made him stop.

'It's a hell of a time since anybody called me that. Don't you think I'm a little old for it?' He grinned boyishly, enchanting her heart, sending her back to the larder to rifle protectively among its shelves as if her life depended on it.

'Well?' came the husky voice at her shoulder.

'Danny, Dan ... I don't want to get involved. I mean—I could easily ... I can't—you know what I'm trying to say. I'm——' She gasped as he fingered the strands of untidy hair that fanned over her cheek. 'Don't ... please. It would only be another notch on the bedpost for you. But for me . . . I don't play around, Daniel. Not any more.'

That much was true at least.

He let his fingers slide away. The severance of their light contact was a physical pain. 'You don't play around . . . any more?' he intoned with a significant glance. 'You did once though, didn't you? Didn't you, Claudia?'

'I—no! I——'

'Liar!'

His eyes narrowed, glinted silver between the long, dark lashes. He was standing so close she could almost count the separate hairs. Memory recalled how she had licked them, with light flicks of the tip of her tongue, joying to feel the flicker of his warm lids against her mouth. But too much had happened since then. Nor should she forget his rejection of her when she had really needed him, though with hindsight, and the maturity the passing years had brought, she could understand why he had acted as he did.

He was measuring out a slow, sardonic appraisal and making no attempt to touch her. It had the sexual impact of the most intimate caress she could imagine. No touching—and she was being touched all over!

'Before we go any further, ma'am, let's get one thing quite straight in our minds. There are no notches on my bedpost.' He moved teasingly closer, so that only a few inches separated them. He could have reached out for her, but must have understood that it wasn't necessary. He was, however, forcing himself to exert control over his own libidinous desires. It was cat and mouse. But she *had* to come to him of her own volition. 'If you don't believe me,' he continued to murmur, saying anything, 'come up and see for yourself.'

'That's not what I've heard or read,' she breathed,

scarcely aware of what she herself was saying. Distantly she remembered some gossip column. A bone of contention. It seemed irrelevant when he was standing this close. 'Countless girlfriends, they accused you of. In the Press. I read it myself.' She tried to say it as if it mattered.

His unwavering look enfolded her in a loving ambience, giving her courage to hope for the first time for something more than she had ever dared.

'Journalists,' he joked, scarcely moving his lips. 'they can spell, but the poor devils never learn to count!' Then he reached out and touched her elbow. 'Come out of the kitchen and drink some of this excellent coffee before it gets cold . . .' He tried to inject some normality into the conversation. It was mainly to preserve himself from going completely overboard and blowing the whole thing with too sudden a declaration. 'I've a feeling we've still a lot of talking to do.' He tried to laugh, but it sounded shaky to his own ears. She was looking at him, almost trusting him with those big blue eyes lapping him up. 'It beats me how we always get side-tracked by one thing or another,' he fibbed, giving a casual glance at his Rolex. It was late. He'd be saved by the bell. 'I have to set off back in a few minutes, but we can finish what we were talking about later, over dinner.'

Claudia sat down shakily, only taking care that she was safely on the opposite side of the table again, out of arm's reach. Her hands were trembling a little as she refilled their coffee-cups, playing hostess. Here loomed the difficult bit. It was like peering over an unimaginably sheer cliff edge.

'Daniel,' she said, reverting deliberately to the more formal version of his name. 'There are things I don't want to go into right now. But it means I can't get involved with anyone.' Least of all you, she wanted to add, but didn't. She kept her eyes on the cup in her hand. 'I suppose I've grown used to independence. It would be a wrench to give it up, and as I've said,' she rushed on, 'I don't play around.'

There was an ominous silence from the other side of the table, and she dared a glance at him, but his face was impassive. He might have been listening to a marginally interesting weather report on the radio for all the emotion he conveyed.

Encouraged, she went on, 'We did agree that we might meet casually now and then in the course of business, or for the odd fun night out——' She gave a weak laugh. 'That's OK by me. I can handle that. But if——'

The crash of a coffee-cup smashing back into its saucer jerked her head upright. A brown stain made the gleaming glass table ugly, then she tried to scramble to her feet as with one stride Daniel cleared the table and pulled her to him. She fell across the back of the chair in her haste to escape, and trembled as his hot breath scoured her face.

'You can cope with a fun night out, can you?' he ground out. 'What's with you, Claudia? Are you living on some other plane we ordinary mortals know nothing about? One minute you're practically seducing me in a public car park, the next you're sitting there like some middle-aged spinster schoolmarm telling me you wouldn't mind the odd fun night out. What do you think I am? A one-man escort agency, bored spinsters for the use of? I leave that sort of thing to the Symeses of this world—though "fun" with him might be stretching the word a bit.' He paused for breath. 'I'd like to break your beautiful neck, Claudia, darling. Do you seriously imagine I'm still a naïve young lad of eighteen you can throw over when you feel like it? You're making a grave mistake if you think you can do that now. It's all or nothing. Do you understand?'

Fear that she would lose control altogether and once more plunge down into the familiar pit of grief when he left her again shook an hysterical peel of laughter from her. 'That's rich coming from you!' she snarled. 'You talk as if *I* left *you*!'

She felt his grip slacken.

'I suppose it makes you feel less of a heel to put it that way to yourself——' she lashed. 'Forget the facts! Forget that I was forced to leave Holcombe and go to live at my aunt's! I didn't choose to go. You know that! You could have written, but you didn't. You could have said something. But you didn't. You could have done something—but you chose to write me out of your life for good! Well, I'll tell you one thing, Daniel Sinnington, although I'm a fool for falling for you, you'll never get me to be that much of a fool again. *That* I promise you!'

Blinding rage made her beat at him with her fists, while his look of stupefaction failed to register. When he spoke it was to say quietly, 'I think your phone's ringing.'

'Damn my phone!' she shouted, despite the reflex that made her reach out to pick it up. It was Susie.

'Yes. I *am* here! I'm coming right down!' She slammed the receiver back. Daniel was still holding her, and she was vibrantly conscious of his hard male body wedged against her own.

'You'd better go,' she rasped.

He glanced at the clock without releasing her. 'Claudia, we've got to talk this through. I don't understand what you're trying to say. I have to go now, so see me tonight——'

Wearily she shook her head.

'Tonight. See me tonight,' he insisted.

'I can't.' Toby was coming home for the weekend.

'Yes, you must.'

'It's impossible.'

'What is there more important than us unravelling this knot of misunderstandings?'

'I happen to have—I have another relationship,' she told him, scarcely daring to breath.

'An important one?'

'Yes.'

She felt his grip slacken a little, but he was still painfully close.

'It's the most important relationship I have,' she went on relentlessly, using Toby as a means of shielding herself.

His grey eyes narrowed slightly. 'Really?'

She nodded. There was a pause. His look told her he didn't quite believe her.

'How long has it been going on?' he asked suspiciously.

'A while.'

'What? Weeks? Months?'

'Years.'

'I see.' There was another pause. 'Not the chap in the car, surely?'

'Certainly not.'

'I see.' Slowly he withdrew his hands from around her waist. 'You should have made it more obvious. I thought there was only that poor devil to be considered—once we'd got the imaginary husband out of the way.' He felt like someone who had run a marathon, only to be told that the finishing line has been moved an indeterminate distance ahead.

He started towards the door. When he reached it he hesitated with his hand on it and turned to look back at her.

'Can't he be put off?' He paused, adding sarcastically, 'This love of your life?'

'He's coming home for the weekend,' she told him deliberately. It sounded as bad as she hoped. He understood—or misunderstood—at once. It made him open the door without saying anything more, and start down the stairs. When he got to the bend he looked back up to where she had come to stand on the landing.

'What am I supposed to say?' he rasped. 'Have a wonderful weekend!'

The anguished note of his wishes was not lost on her.

'You, too,' she added in a whisper after his retreating back. 'You, too.'

Feeling utterly wretched, she watched him disappear from sight. It was best this way, she told herself, as her heart lay in a thousand fragments at her feet.

CHAPTER FIVE

SUSIE was all apologies as she walked into reception a few minutes later.

'I'm sorry, love. It hadn't crossed my mind you'd got somebody up there with you,' she began.

'What do you mean?' Claudia exclaimed.

If she hoped to persuade Susie that she had been alone in the flat she was on a loser.

Susie said as much, confessing almost at once what she imagined had been going on, adding 'I don't normally hallucinate tall blond hunks like Daniel Sinnington hurtling through reception first thing in the morning!'

'Oh,' replied Claudia tonelessly.

'Is that all you've got to say, "oh"?' demanded Susie grinning her head off at Claudia's discomfort. Then, catching sight of her set expression she immediately frowned. 'Sorry! I'm opening my big mouth as usual. So you finished up with a bit of a tiff. Never mind! I'm sure it's all worth it for one night with him!'

'Susie! For heaven's sake!' Claudia blushed scarlet and felt for all the world like a teenager caught hand in hand with her first boyfriend. 'It wasn't like that at all. He simply called by this morning——'

Susie's expression was a picture of disbelief.

'It's true! I spent the night at Lake House. Ask Peter, if you don't believe me! He dropped me off last night after supper——'

'You mean you turned *Daniel* down for——' Susie bit her lip. It wasn't for her to criticise how Claudia ran her lovelife, but she couldn't help adding, 'Claudia, sometimes I think you're quite mad!' She shot her an exasperated look. 'What on earth's going on, then? I don't get it.' Her brow puckered. 'I mean, seriously, you've been very tense ever since Daniel Sinnington came on the scene. Almost as if you hate him. But he's a gorgeous guy and he's obviously interested in you—how on earth can you send such a guy packing? When he came through here just now his face was like a thunder cloud!'

'Probably because he's not going to get everything all his own way,' retorted Claudia, trying to appear cool. 'I don't like being waylaid in the car park before I even have chance to open my eyes!' She was trying to make light of the incident, praying that Susie would drop the matter. But Susie gave her a shrewd glance.

'You can talk to me, you know, love. We go back quite a long way. I know I have a big mouth, but for anything important—well,' she shrugged, 'you know I'm available for tea and sympathy.'

Claudia bit her lip. Susie had got it in one. She needed desperately to talk to somebody sympathetic, if only to try to get things clear in her own mind. She didn't expect advice from anyone else, because only she knew the full story and what she had to do. It's just that it was beginning to drive her up the wall. To talk, maybe joke a little, would ease her turmoil.

She returned her look with a rueful smile. 'It's not that I don't want to trust you—I know you wouldn't deliberately let anything slip if it was in confidence—it's just that it's something difficult to talk about.' Her voice was scarcely audible as she continued, 'Something happened a long time ago. I don't want to go raking it all up. It—it still hurts.'

'You mean you've met Daniel before?' puzzled Susie.

'Yes.' Claudia clenched her fists, wanting to share her

troubles, but frightened to risk undermining the sense of security she had managed to build up over the years.

'How old were you when you—when you knew him the first time around?' Susie enquired tentatively.

'Seventeen,' muttered Claudia, flinching a little as the past came rushing back like a devouring demon.

Susie gave a sympathetic grimace. 'I see . . .' She patted Claudia on the arm. 'Come on. I'll make a cup of coffee. There's nothing booked till ten.'

She went through into the small room they used as a kitchen and popped the kettle on, emerging a few seconds later with cups and saucers, while Claudia made delaying sounds even as she sat herself down on the edge of the desk and toyed with the pencils neatly arrayed in the slim glass container beside Susie's perennial vase of flowers. Maybe it was true—she had allowed herself to become burdened down with the desire to talk, and now everything to do with Daniel Sinnington seemed loaded with danger. To talk, even casually, would help put things into perspective.

Even so, she still found it difficult to start. 'There's really nothing to tell,' she began, 'we just happened to go out together for a few weeks one summer . . .'

'First love? All that?' prompted Susie. 'And you fell for him, hook, line and sinker?'

Even now Claudia could blush at the memory of her passion for him. It would have been nice to be able to dismiss it like that, with a nonchalant shrug, first love— all that! She didn't reply.

Susie gave a grimace of sympathy. 'I guess we all go through it at some time.'

Claudia bit her lip. 'Most people get over it.'

'If it ended badly,' Susie wasn't probing, merely offering her immediate interpretation, 'then it must have been a shock to bump into him suddenly like that.'

Claudia gazed off into the distance, her brow creased. 'I seem to have lost all sense of humour over him, don't I?' she fretted.

'It's hitting you hard, that's all. You'll be as right as rain in a couple of days.' She hesitated, then went on, 'I still don't see why you can't let bygones be bygones and take up where you left off. He's obviously changed his mind about you—and you can't deny he's quite a dish. What is there to lose by being nice and friendly to each other?'

Claudia gave a harsh laugh. There was plenty to lose! But it was something she could never divulge to Susie, or to anyone. But Susie's interest was aroused now, and Claudia felt compelled to offer some explanation. Prompted by the unaccustomed relief of talking about her private self, she began. 'Everything was fine until I was seventeen——' She paused.

'Go on,' encouraged Susie, eyeing her sympathetically over the rim of her coffee-cup.

'Then everything seemed to go wrong at once ... It started when Mother died very suddenly. We'd been really close. Father had always been away a lot. Suddenly to be without her—well, you can imagine, at that age it leaves you with only your friends for support—at least, that's how it was for me.' She bit her lip and gazed back into the past with a small frown. 'Father was always away—abroad—and when he *was* around he never seemed at all interested. Now, of course, I realise it was his nature. He was a cold, selfish man. But at that time I used to feel guilty—it was *my* fault he wasn't nice to me, and his rejection of Mum was somehow my fault, too!' She gave a little laugh. 'It seems silly now.' Then she gave Susie a quick glance. I'm sorry. It's not especially sensational, is it?'

She tried to laugh it of, but Susie pushed the biscuit

tin towards her and told her, 'Love, if it hurt, and if it can hurt now, it *is* important, because *you're* important. So stop belittling what you feel. I'd guess you've never really given yourself the chance to talk it out to anybody, and that's wrong. You mustn't be so hard on yourself when you've got friends. This is what friends are for . . .'

'I did talk it out—once,' Claudia corrected slowly, conscious that she was about to admit to a part of her life that had been repressed for years. 'I talked it out with Daniel. We used to have long talks beside the swimming pool at his house, when all the rest of the gang had gone home. There was a crowd of us that summer. But I was closest to him. He let me talk about what Father did next—at the time it seemed unforgivable. I felt devastated. And Dan understood . . .' She gave Susie a wry glance. 'Father remarried about three weeks after mother's funeral. To a woman I thought had been one of her best friends . . . so much for friendship! It seemed such a horrible thing to do. As if they'd both been waiting for her to die. Of course, I know that wasn't true. I suppose she just happened to be there when he was feeling at his most vulnerable.' She gave a short laugh. 'At seventeen, you find it difficult to imagine that parents can be allowed weaknesses, too. I just felt shattered. I was still in mourning for Mother. I thought he should be, too. I felt so alone . . . except, of course, for Daniel.'

'What was he like then?'

'Perfect,' she replied simply, then laughed. 'I didn't learn my lesson after what Father did. It should have made me more cautious where men are concerned. But it didn't. I really thought Dan was perfect. I transferred all my hero worship from Dad to Daniel. What a burden for an eighteen-year-old!'

She shrugged and gave a faint smile.

'Everybody was crazy about him. But he scarcely seemed to notice the effect he had. His people had bought a vast house set in its own woodland just outside the village, so he was new to the area. Golly, how we used to giggle over his name, Sinnington!' She paused. 'At first he hardly registered with me. When everybody used to swoon over him, I used to think to myself, what idiots they are! Not really seeing him as a real person. I suppose there was just too much going on at home. Then, just as we were becoming friends, Father dropped his second bombshell—he decided to go back to South America—he was working for a company out there— taking the new wife with him. But, and this was it, he didn't want *me* with them. He arranged for me to be packed off to an aunt I'd never met!' She shrugged. 'I was given no say in the matter, despite the fact that I was in the middle of my final exam year. Being uprooted meant changing syllabus—you know, there was all that sort of thing. But he didn't care a damn. It suited him to parcel me off to somebody else. So that's what happened. In the mean time, I poured all this out to Dan. He was super. I really believed I could trust him. We seemed to become real friends. And of course, I began to fall in love.'

'So what went wrong?' asked Susie, looking puzzled. 'Did you go to the aunt's? Is that what brought your friendship to a stop?'

'Eventually, yes, I went to live with her. But Daniel and I parted before that—he went off on holiday with his folks, words of undying love on his lips . . .' She gave a cynical smile. 'Well, he was young, wasn't he? What else would he have said? The trouble was, by this time I was hopelessly involved with him. It could only have been because he'd stood by me, or so I thought, all through that summer. I went through a phase of getting into all kinds of scrapes. An attention getting thing I suppose. But Dan always brought me down to earth. Helped me get rid of a lot of anger I felt towards Father ...' She grimaced. 'Daniel's charm, even then, was quite devastating. He must have been born with it. He'd certainly learned how to use it by the time he turned it on me. He made me feel as if I was the most wonderful person in the world.' Her voice took on a bitter note. 'I thought I could trust him.'

'And you couldn't?'

'Is anybody to be trusted?'

'Yes, I believe they are.'

'I'd rather not risk it, thanks.'

'Oh, Claudia ...' Susie's kind face clouded over. 'He must have let you down very badly.'

'No,' Claudia denied quickly, too quickly, thought Susie. 'He was only eighteen. I simply expected too much. We were both so young.' She ran a hand through the sleek dark hair, and then gave a dismissive shrug, as if the load had been moved from off her shoulders merely by talking about it. Of course, it hadn't worked. She had been right to be reluctant to unburden herself in this weak and spineless way. What good could talking do?

Susie leaned forward. 'What happened next?'

Claudia gave a quickly concealed jump. 'Nothing,' she answered shortly.

'Nothing?'

'Nothing.' When she chanced a glance, Susie was eyeing her carefully.

'Now you've met up with him again, everything should be rainbows. You surely can't bear a grudge against him after all this time?' She hesitated, as if conscious of the dangerous ground she was treading

'Susie, I love you dearly, but you sometimes have an

annoying habit of stating the obvious. Rainbows it's not.'

'So if not, why not?' she persisted, not at all put down by Claudia's obvious desire to dismiss her curiosity out of hand. There was a long pause in which Claudia struggled with the desire to tip her cup of coffee over Susie's head, or to blurt out every last little detail in a final splurge of truth-telling.

But, grinning infuriatingly, Susie pre-empted her by saying, 'OK, Mrs Gray, you're off the hook for the time being, but don't think I'm going to be satisfied with only half a story. You know me, if net curtains didn't exist, I'd be the one to invent them.'

'You're damned right,' rejoined Claudia humorously, recovering her self-possession at the same time, 'Ever thought of getting a job with MI5? You could run the show single-handed.'

Susie smiled broadly. 'I'll get the spotlights rigged for next time and a new tape in the recorder.'

'It'd make riveting play-back. You could market it as a sleep tape.' Claudia picked up their two cups and hid herself in the cubby-hole where they did the washing-up. Despite the ribbing, she wondered just how much Susie would really suspect once her mind got to work on her story. For of course, that wasn't all, and Susie was quite capable of putting two and two together.

The weekend—the 'wonderful weekend' she had been ordered to have with such sarcasm—was half over. If it hadn't been utterly wonderful—for she ruefully admitted, only one person could make her weekends truly wonderful—then it had at least been as varied and enjoyable as anyone had a right to expect.

She spent Saturday morning working in the salon— only getting off early when Susie volunteered to take over, so Claudia could spend the rest of the day with Toby doing the last-minute chores for the barbecue that evening.

'I'm so glad you phoned the final numbers through to Susie when you did,' she told Toby as they loaded up the boot of the car with last-minute shopping. 'I was only going to cater for twenty!'

'Twenty? Honestly! What sort of barbecue would that be?' Toby scoffed. He had manfully lugged stuff from the freezer centre and, when they got home, set about organising the charcoal and the grid-irons and all the other necessary bits and pieces for the barbecue in the paved-off area half-way down the garden.

'I don't want you to get too involved with the fire-raising side!' she told him humorously, later. 'Leave that to me. You just concentrate on making sure your friends are having a good time.'

'You've got to have a good time too, you know.'

She reached up and ruffled his blond hair. 'I will. Bet your cotton socks!'

'Peter coming over, is he?' The question was offhand. It didn't seem to follow on from their previous lines about having a good time. An echo of yesterday's conversation with Daniel made her scowl briefly. He was already putting doubts into her mind. He and Susie between them. And now, possibly Toby as well. What was the general opinion—that Peter and fun were mutually exclusive?

She pushed Toby outside. 'He may come over. He may not.' She pretended not to notice Toby's grimace. 'And leave the matches alone. I'm quite capable of lighting a barbecue, thanks very much.'

It was nearly over now. There had been well over twenty guests—more like eighty—and each with the appetite of ten. Luckily she had overbought, remembering previous occasions, and she had had the forethought to make an enormous pan of soup to see everyone on their way when things began to wind down.

With a quick once-over to make sure that everyone was provided for, she went back inside to the kitchen to put the pan on the hob. Peter was standing at the window, a glass of wine in one hand. He didn't offer to help as she piled a large wedge of butter on to a dish with a couple of salt cellars and some mayonnaise and—she puckered her brow, what else had Toby asked for?— mustard, that was it, then proceeded to carry the whole lot out to the waiting hordes.

The garden looked a treat now, with fairy-lights dotted among the trees, and one or two garden flares lighting up strategic parts of the shrubbery. A glance towards the house itself showed that it looked very inviting, with the french windows standing open and a subdued pinkish glow coming from within. For once it looks like the family house it was, and to complete the picture there should have been someone somewhere inside to share the everyday joy and heartache, too. A deeply concealed well of emptiness suddenly opened up at her feet. Shaking the mood off, Claudia tried to count her blessings as she moved down the gracefully unfolding lawns to the crowd standing around the barbecue. It was astonishing, she told herself, that none of Toby's friends had thrown either themselves or each other into the water. He had told her they were a good bunch, but she had been sceptical. At least the neighbours would be impressed by their decorum. She had been careful to invite the one or two couples whose property shared the lake frontage with her, but none of them had turned up.

Secretly she was relieved, even while she regretted the

lack of warm-heartedness in the little lakeside community. Still, it was what she had actively sought—the anonymity of a respectable life-style. No questions asked.

This evening of all evenings she was conscious how much she needed that—because more than ever she was conscious of being an imposter. The recent memory of Daniel's touch on her skin—his engulfing kiss in the car park and her blatant surrender to it—brought fantasies that were anything but respectable.

As she walked across the grass she gave a quick review of the figures adorning the garden benches, then she nearly dropped the tray with shock. An audible gasp escaped her lips. At that precise moment a tall, lithe figure had detached itself from the shadows by the wall where the path that ran round the side of the house came out below the terrace, and even now was striding purposefully across the lawn towards her. She blinked twice, sure she must be dreaming.

By the time he reached her, the baked potatoes had already been observed and she was surrounded by an army of Toby's friends, so that instead of being able to let rip with the full force of her anger at his audacity in actually gate-crashing Toby's barbecue, all she could do was squeak his name.

'Daniel!' then, weakly, she managed, 'What are you doing *here*?'

'Claudia!' He mimicked her surprise. 'Come here often?' His eyes glinted in anything but a friendly fashion, as if he had caught her red-handed at something shameful.

Her mind went blank of all the saucy rejoinders she could have employed, and she felt her jaw sag stupidly while eager hands depleted the serving bowls of their hot potatoes.

'Am I gate-crashing?' he asked, with an imperturbable smile curving his desirable lips.

Striving to remain unmoved she clipped, 'Yes,' and then stopped, all other words having drained from her mind.

'That's bad,' he replied comfortably.

Striving to recover from the shock of seeing him, she blurted, 'How—how did you find out where I was?'

'Persistence and charm,' he retorted confidently. 'Weapons I didn't know how to use thirteen years ago.'

'Look——' She glanced wildly around. Their conversation was taking place so publicly, though nobody seemed to be much interested in it, that she was desperate to get him away, out of earshot, before he said anything too outrageous. 'This is no good—I can't talk to you here. Can't you see I'm busy?'

'You look adorable surrounded by all these young Turks. You ought to have some of your own!'

'For heaven's sake!' She wanted to throw the tray at him, but he would probably throw it back. The ground seemed to be opening up at her feet again.

'Go away,' she ordered half-heartedly.

'No.'

'Well, that's that settled, isn't it?' With a grim smile she strode purposefully towards the barbecue in order to get rid of what remained of the baked potatoes. Toby came up, all smiles.

'I'm glad you've invited somebody decent.'

'Decent? Who's decent?'

'Your friend. The one who's just arrived.'

'How do you know he's decent?'

'He looks it.'

'Don't be taken in by the façade.'

'I'll give him a drink so I can check him out.'

'*Don't you dare!* See to your own guests, please!' The

force of her expression took him by surprise.

'Yes, ma'am!' he saluted smartly, then dodged away, grinning vilely, before she could catch him.

Please, please dear God, she prayed as she made her way back across the grass, let them all do as I want. She noticed that Peter was still standing at the kitchen window, gazing out in a lordly, rather proprietorial manner. Stay there, she silently commanded.

Then she turned her attention to Daniel, who was standing in the middle of the lawn looking round as if the whole scene would probably dematerialise at any minute. All she had to do was persuade him to leave. All? she thought wryly.

'I can't imagine what you think you're doing here!' she attacked as soon as they were out of earshot of the others. Her momentary relief that he had come bursting back into her life, even after his last parting shot, had given way to the old urge to run.

Of course, there was no running. She was trapped like a rabbit in its hole by a fox. Under the pretence of leading him into the house, she managed to get him back on to the terrace to a part that was out of sight of the kitchen. As it happened to be close to the open french windows, she adroitly shepherded him inside.

'What I think I'm doing here and what I'm actually doing here may turn out to be the same thing,' he told her enigmatically as he followed her lead into the sitting-room. 'But I must admit, teenage barbecues are not my usual scene these days,' he informed her, with an amused smile, 'and I didn't think they were yours, either.'

She stopped abruptly in the shadowy sitting-room that not five minutes ago had looked so warm and inviting. Now her senses crackled with the prospect of danger.

He gave her a lazy glance from beneath straight brows, his eyes glinting with some unspoken emotion.

'I was also dying of curiosity to see who or what it was that was making my own weekend so dull.' He laid an arm around her waist before she could stop him. 'Claudia, your eyes don't lie. You're as shaken up by what's happening between us as I am. Admit it.'

She gulped. The desire to rest her head on his shoulder and succumb to the magic of his touch nearly overwhelmed her good sense, but the proximity of Toby and co, as well as Peter, made her draw back with a start of alarm. There was too much at stake to throw it all away on a weakness for Daniel's practised charm.

'You should never have come here uninvited,' she told him ferociously.

'I've done a lot of things in my life I probably shouldn't have. Invited as well as uninvited,' he added in a voice all milk and honey. 'You want apologies? You've come to the wrong man.'

'I don't want apologies. I want you to go. Now!'

'Very welcoming!'

For a moment, in the half-light, she thought she saw a flicker of some other feeling beneath the steel-edged tones that sent her own feelings into such a turmoil, but his honeying humorous manner came back straight away

'Look at it my way, Claudia. I've taken the trouble to sleuth out here after you on a Saturday night, instead of living it up in some fashionable night-spot with one of my—what was it?—countless girlfriends, and now you're going to turn me out without even a hot potato, let alone anything stronger for my trouble.'

'Gate-crashers deserve all they get—or in this case, all they don't get,' she hit back, refusing to succumb.

'Not even half a glass of wine and a stroll by the lakeside?'

'No.'

He pulled a face. 'Your friends have a beautiful place here—wouldn't they like you to show me round?'

'It's not on the market.' She felt light-headed with the ramifications his words had opened up. Friends? He thought she was a guest of friends?

'Where are they, by the way?' he went on. 'Shouldn't you introduce me as your long-lost lover? I'd feel less like a gate-crasher that way——'

'Daniel!' There was reproof in her tone, but she agonised at the casual accuracy of his words.

'Is it such an outrageous suggestion? Or is there something I don't know that makes you so unreasonable?'

This second bull's eye had her blazing round at him, losing all control. 'Peter's here with me! What will he think if I go smooching round the lake with you?'

'Who said anything about smooching? Although now you've put the idea into my head——'

'Daniel! Are you *never* serious?' She was almost crying with frustration. Any minute now Peter, or worse, Toby, would come barging in. If the former, things would be stiffly unpleasant, but she could probably handle that. If the latter, however, chasms of horrid possibilities opened up before her.

Just then a troop of Toby's friends started to amble across the lawn to the house, shouting their goodbyes as they did so.

Moving quickly towards the french windows, she ordered, 'Wait here. Have a Scotch or something. I'll be with you in a moment.'

Before he could protest, she ran lightly down to the group walking on to the terrace in order to forstall them.

'All off now?' she called out, slipping back into her earlier role. A fleeting glance showed her that Daniel had miraculously done as she had suggested. His shape was outlined briefly in the pinkish glow from a floor lamp as he moved across the room to the drinks cabinet.

A few minutes later, having given strict instructions to Toby not to disturb her, she rejoined him.

'Everybody seems to be leaving now.' She remarked. 'How about following suit?' She regarded him coolly, although her heart was thumping frantically at the thought of what he might do next.

He turned at the sound of her voice and gazed across at her from his place in the shadows of the winged leather armchair. As their eyes met and held, there was a palpable pause. His hair was the brightest patch of colour in the sombre furnishings of the room, she noted. It felt as if a hundred years had passed—time seemed to wing past, making her conscious of the ebb and flow of tides, the world revolving on its axis and stars taking light years to move across the fields of heaven . . . This is what love is! she registered in bewilderment. This is what it has always been.

He was staring at her so intently she could imagine he was able to read her thoughts. The idea frightened her. She could never allow anyone to get that close, least of all, Daniel.

'Well,' he spoke smoothly, breaking the silence hardly at all, 'You *are* keen to get rid of me. I wonder why?'

'Because you look as if you belong there in that chair,' she admitted helplessly.

'Perhaps I do,' he replied at once with a quirk of his lips.

'No.' She raised a hand as it to fend off the thought, then more urgently added, 'What would people think if they saw you here?'

'They'd think I was your lover—your man,' he teased gently.

'I've already got one—a man,' she hastened to correct. 'He's drinking white wine in the kitchen. I'd hate to be seen as someone claiming more than my fair share.'

'Ignore them. They're only jealous.' He smiled the silvery smile that did such strange things to her will-power, and contemplated the amber liquid in his glass. 'I don't feel guilty about drinking someone else's Scotch, so why should you feel guilty about entertaining two men in someone else's home? You obviously have understanding friends—either that or they're scared of teenagers. Why have they all left so soon, by the way?'

'It's not soon. It's midnight. They've all gone back to school.'

'Night school?'

'Boarding school. It was a mass exeat for the barbecue. And they're scarcely teenagers.'

'How did you get yourself roped in?'

'Forget it. Just go.'

'Friendly as ever. Where are my hosts? I want to thank them for their hospitality. And meet my rival,' he added calmly.

'I think they'd rather you left without causing trouble,' she managed to breathe.

'I assure you I have no intention of causing trouble. Anything but. In fact, to prove it, I'll help you go round the garden dowsing the flares before they set any more bushes on fire.'

'What?' She spun to the window but, as she should have realised, all was well, and Daniel's throaty chuckle sent her turning on him, eyes blazing. But he was already looking towards the sitting-room door, which was slowly swinging open to admit a dark shape silhouetted in the light from the hall.

Claudia felt suddenly sick with apprehension, until she saw that it was only Peter.

'Claudia, I wondered where on earth you'd got to—oh!' he stopped abruptly. 'I didn't know you were with someone.' He faltered on the threshold, obviously recognising Daniel from the previous evening, and at a loss to make out what he was doing sitting at ease in one of Claudia's armchairs.

'You're just off, are you?' cut in Daniel jauntily before Claudia could stop him.

'I—I suppose so,' Peter looked nonplussed, as well he might.

Claudia held her breath. Did she or did she not want to interfere? It would simplify life if Peter went right now, because she couldn't guarantee that he wouldn't say something to alert Daniel's suspicious mind. On the other hand, she didn't relish the prospect of being left alone with Daniel. He was too hot to handle at the best of times—and tonight he was like a simmering volcano, despite his urbane manner.

'It is quite latish, actually.' Peter peered at his watch, taking the initiative from her. 'I thought I'd probably start to make tracks, though perhaps——' He paused '—perhaps I should offer to lend a hand with the clearing up?'

'No——'

'Don't bother, old chap.'

Daniel and Claudia both spoke at once.

'I'll give Claudia a hand if you've got to get off,' Daniel continued smoothly. He remained firmly in his armchair. The victor enthroned, thought Claudia maliciously. What a pity she was in agreement with this concealed order to Peter, otherwise she would have had great delight in telling him where he could get off.

She moved towards the door, and with a mixture of

relief and irritation watched Peter allow her to edge him unprotestingly homewards.

As he pulled on his overcoat and began to button it up, she asked, 'Have you bumped into Toby in the last ten minutes?'

He grimaced. 'I heard a small army of them going upstairs a short while ago.'

'Good. Sounds as if they've gone off to bed.'

'And so shall I, my dear.' He bent to kiss her lightly on the lips. 'Not quite my cup of tea, this evening, but never mind.'

'Thank you for your support.' Even if it did amount to standing on the fringes, downing wine, she added silently.

At last she was able to close the door behind him. She leaned against it for a second or two, and tried to clear her head.

With a deep breath she approached the cause of all her misgivings. He was beside the french windows, looking out at the garden when she came in, standing very still, with the half-full glass in his hand, and turning to greet her with a quizzical smile at the sound of her entrance.

'Are you holding the fort here all by yourself?' he queried, handing her a glass of Scotch as she came up beside him.

'Yes,' she began, intending to ask him to leave as soon as he had finished his drink.

But he continued. 'It's a strange way to spend a Saturday night, isn't it? I imagined you in much more sophisticated circumstances.'

'You don't really know me, Daniel. I've changed.'

'No one changes out of all recognition—unless something pretty dire happens to them.' His grey eyes sparkled over her trim, still youthful form, in its hip-hugging blue jeans and simple white T-shirt that revealed the once young curves in all their maturity. She blushed self-consciously. First at his words, and secondly at the unmistakable expression on his face. Without the protective gloss she wore for her job, she felt naked beneath his scrutiny.

'Dire?' She gave a hard laugh to cover her confusion. 'Now what would you consider dire enough to change me, I wonder?' Bitterness that he could say such a thing filled her heart. But she added, as casually as she could, 'The only thing that has happened to me in the last so many years is that I've grown up.'

'Come for a drive,' he suggested abruptly.

'What? Now?'

'Now, Claudia. Of course now! I'll drive you home afterwards.'

'Are you mad? I've got four boys to babysit. I can't just go off and leave them!'

'I didn't realise it was an all-night job. Why can't your friends babysit their own boys?'

When she didn't answer he asked, 'I suppose they'll burn the house down if you go out?'

'Probably,' she replied shortly.

Now that everyone had left, and they both knew it, the silence of the house took on a different meaning. It made her shiver. The air seemed full of secrets, and full of possibilities that made her draw in her breath with alarm. Once again she felt like an imposter, but added to that was the urgent fear that her mask would be snatched away.

Falling back on the old standby, she turned away. 'I'm tired,' she informed him. 'It's been a long evening.'

Daniel wasn't taken in. 'I thought it was traditional for babysitters to entertain their boyfriends until the parents came back?'

'I'm not sixteen, Daniel. One doesn't have boyfriends at my age.'

'No? Then one should.' He moved closer.

'How do you know so much about babysitters, anyway?' she attacked quickly, drawing back as if looking at something out of the window.

'Not first-hand experience, if that's what you're angling to find out. I don't have any children, and when I do I intend to be married to their mother.'

Claudia shivered and moved to the windows to close them. It was a mistake, because he didn't get out of the way as she had expected when she leaned forward to fasten the catch, but instead put his hand over the back of hers as she turned the key in the lock.

'What time are they coming back?' he murmured into the hair on her neck.

'Late,' she lied, then realised it was a mistake.

He laughed softly. 'Good—the later the better!' His hand pressured hers as she withdrew the key from the lock. She heard the soft metallic sound of it as it slipped to the parquet floor, then somehow or other his arms were around her.

'No! You must go,' she muttered, not daring to move at all.

'You look seventeen tonight, Claudia,' he said, hushing her. 'No make-up. Untidy hair. Wide, beautiful, innocent yes.' His lips were hovering just above her own, then they came down on hers, warm, exploratory pressing softly. She felt her limbs acquire the softness of feathers, and somehow or other she was nestling back among the plumped-up cushions of the sofa, with the hard long length of his body reviving her own with his blazing vitality.

'I don't want to love you, Daniel. I can't——' she told him hoarsely.

'I know. But I'm going to teach you how—like I did the first time.' His eyes gleamed wickedly between the long, dark lashes.

'You think all you have to do is to persuade me to give in, and you joke about it all the time, as if it doesn't really matter, as if love's a joke. But it won't work this time, Daniel, because I'm wise to your technique now.' She wondered why she was arguing with him, as if it was a skirmish before surrendering to him. He must have thought the same, because when she pushed him away, he moved aside without argument. Once again she felt like an imposter as she adopted a haughty tone of voice to say, 'I find this scrambling around on a sofa most undignified.' She rose to her feet.

'What are you suggesting, Claudia?' He looked faintly startled.

She pursed her lips in genuine annoyance. '*Not* what you imagine!' She moved towards the fireplace and leaned against it. 'I want you to leave.'

It was her turn to be startled, for he disentangled his long limbs from among the cushions on the sofa and stood up at once.

'Don't worry. I wouldn't compromise you in front of your friends.' His tone was faintly derisory, and for a fleeting moment she wondered what she had done to cause this abrupt reversal. He wasn't usually so instantly amenable.

'I tracked you down because I wanted to talk to you,' he explained. 'Not because I was looking for a quick grope on a sofa.' The savage dismissal of the apparent tenderness he had felt only a moment before shocked her and she could only gape as he went on, 'I also rather looked forward to a confrontation with the most important man in your life.' When he noticed the vaguely puzzled expression on her face, he elaborated,

'You know—the one you tried to scare me off with yesterday morning! Remember?'

Claudia's senses were immediately alerted and she realised that it had been a mistake to drop her guard at all—despite his bantering mood, there was more to Daniel Sinnington than sweet innocence. Scorched by guilt, feeling the revelations she dreaded were imminent, she could only stare up at him—like a victim waiting for the knife. He straddled an upright chair beside the bureau and smiled blandly across at her.

'Right,' he began smoothly, 'where have we got to so far, Mrs Hampshire? Or is it Miss or Ms these days? I assume our recently departed friend is not the love of your life, so where is he? Who is he? And what's his name?'

'Leave it, will you?' she gasped, unable to think straight. 'It's got nothing to do with you!'

'I will not leave it until I'm good and ready. And if it's got nothing to do with me now, I'll *make* it have something to do with me!'

She noticed how white his knuckles shone as he gripped the back of the chair, but his voice was relaxed, cool, as he enumerated the possible reasons for her secrecy.

'Who owns this house, Claudia? Is it your lover—this so-important figure in your life? If so, why isn't he here by your side, protecting you from the intrusions of men like me?' He laughed abruptly. 'Or is he only a part-time lover? Married, perhaps? So you have to spend your Saturday nights babysitting for friends?'

'You're raving, Daniel. None of this is true!'

'Then tell me what *is* true, damn you!'

'For the last time, my personal life has nothing to do with you! If you ever had a reason to know anything about me, you forfeited that right years ago! Now get out!' Realising that she was beginning to shout, she lowered her voice. 'Please, Daniel. I don't want this!'

'I think the truth is beginning to fall into place.' He went on as if she hadn't spoken. 'There is no husband, for a start. We've agreed on that. Right so far?'

'OK. Gray is my business name. Now, will you go?' she came back, voice rising again.

'Not until I've got to the bottom of it all. You can't keep on running away from the idea of us, Claudia. I won't allow it!'

Panic made her rise to her feet. 'What right have you to come here and start grilling me as if I'm in the dock?' She advanced on him with eyes of blue flame. 'I didn't invite you here, and now I'm tired. I've had a long day and I want to go to bed—alone,' she emphasised before he could comment.

But he was no longer in a bantering mood. Catching her by the wrist, he pulled her down close and hissed, 'What's the matter with you, Claudia? What have you to hide?'

'N-nothing. Why should I hide anything?'

'You don't want to admit to the existence of a lover who owns all this—is that it?' He repeated his earlier accusation, which she had ignored.

'I don't want you prying into my life. Get out!' she whispered hoarsely, as she thought she heard a sound from upstairs. Twisting away from him, she almost managed to pull free, but he caught hold of her wrists and held them for a moment with a look of murderous intent on his face, then abruptly he released her.

Running a hand violently through his short blond hair, so that the familiar straight lock fell over his forehead again, he growled, 'I could shake the truth out of you, but is it worth it?' He gave her a withering look. 'If secrecy is so precious to you, keep it. Who am I to pry? If you want to deny what exists between us, go ahead. May you live to regret it, Claudia. I certainly shan't——' He rose rapidly to his feet. 'I guess I'm well out of the situation. There's something very wrong—and your silence can only mean that it's something I wouldn't want to know!'

In three short strides he was at the door. 'I'm sorry I gate-crashed the party. Not my style. You're welcome to your secret lover, Claudia, whoever he is. And you're right. It's nothing to do with me.' He paused. 'Back to how we were. OK? Try not to forget our meeting at ten sharp on Monday to discuss the décor. If it's not convenient——' he shrugged '—let's forget the whole damned business!'

She watched the door close behind him, and then a few seconds later heard the slight slam of the front door as he let himself out.

Very, very slowly she released a long sighing breath and unclenched her fingers. She was saved. At least, she had saved herself in the way she thought was best. But, in another way, she knew she was tasting the bitter fruits of defeat.

CHAPTER SIX

'ALL right, Susie! You've got some explaining to do!' It was Monday morning. Claudia was lying in wait, and pounced as soon as Susie showed her face. Her startled expression did nothing to halt Claudia's rapid attack.

'How did that man track me down to Lake House? Who told him where I would be on Saturday night? Why, Susie? Why did you do it?'

She passed a hand over her brow, conscious that her anger had grown ever since she had started to puzzle out how Daniel had come to make his unexpected appearance at the barbecue. 'Complications are what I *don't* need. Especially from a man like that!' she stormed, before Susie could think up a defence. 'I want nothing to do with him. Don't you understand? What I told you about the things that happened in the past—it should have made it obvious I don't want him in my life again. A complete idiot could surely understand that? How *could* you do it, Susie? How could you betray me?'

'Claudia, wait—it wasn't quite like that,' broke in Susie defensively. 'He turned up here on Saturday morning just after you'd left. You went off early, remember?'

'So? You promptly gave him my private address?' Claudia gave a disgusted look.

'No!' exclaimed Susie. 'Well,' she added apologetically, 'not straight away.' She bit her lip. 'Honestly, I'm sorry if I've caused trouble. I didn't mean to. I genuinely thought you'd invited him to Toby's barbecue.' She furrowed her brow. 'That's the impression he gave me, anyway. I mean, he seemed surprised that you'd already left when he called, so I assumed you'd forgotten that you'd arranged to meet him——'

'Crazy!' Claudia shook her head wonderingly.

'Then, somehow, chatting, it just seemed natural to mention what you were doing. You know how it is, Claudia, chatting to a guy like that——'

'Oh, yes,' Claudia nodded, her anger, after its initial explosion, already seeming futile.

But Susie was eager to expiate herself. 'Honestly, he implied that he knew all about it, but he'd declined because he had some other engagement, and then managed to drop that one in favour of yours. He wasn't quite sure how to get to Lake House, he said, so I told him. Nothing nefarious about it! At least, not on my part.' She eyed Claudia cautiously, as if not sure whether her anger had really abated or whether she was due for a further more lethal outburst.

Claudia smiled weakly. 'OK. He could charm anything out of anyone. Why should you be immune? I'm not. Not quite.' She felt cold as a thought struck her. 'What did he say when he knew it was Toby's barbecue? Did he ask who Toby was?'

Susie frowned. 'No. I don't think we actually mentioned Toby by name . . . I assumed he knew.'

'Well, I can tell you something, Susie, he knows *nothing* about my personal life, despite his constant prying, and that's the way I want it to stay. Understand?'

Susie looked bemused and gave a small shrug. 'OK. I'm sorry. You know I always put my foot in it if it's humanly possible.

Remembering Daniel's own words about how he'd

used a mixture of charm and persistence in order to track her down, she felt a twinge of remorse at taking such a high-handed attitude to poor Susie.

'Who could resist him?' she apologised for her outburst. 'He can be damned persuasive when he wants to be——' Blushing, she recalled his touch on her skin, his eyes, drawing her to him as if she had no will of her own. After his parting words on Saturday night there might be no need to issue any sort of warning to Susie— he had given up, he'd said—but Claudia was now so thoroughly on edge she didn't believe a word he told her. Susie, warned, would at least give her a little more peace of mind.

Verbally pinned against the door from the moment she had arrived, Susie now came on into reception and deposited her bag on the desk before untying her coat.

'It must have been a shock for him when he saw the place, and the kids and all.' She giggled. 'How did he take it?'

Claudia turned away, pretending to be busy. 'He seems to have a tendency to jump to conclusions,' she hinted, 'and he rather got the idea I was babysitting for friends.' She shot Susie a look of complicity for which no words were needed.

Susie giggled again. 'Don't worry. I won't let on. Though how long you think you can get away with it, I can't imagine!'

'It's simpler that way,' Claudia faltered, hating the web of lies and hating more that she should start to involve anyone else. But she added. 'He's a playboy— you've read the gossip columns yourself. I just don't want to get involved.'

'I understand, love. Such a waste, though! Still, I can see your point. He's safer at a distance!'

'Some distance!' Claudia observed. 'I now have to spend the rest of the morning cooped up with him in his office discussing décor!'

Claudia gunned her sports car out on to the ring road and there was troubled frown on her face as Susie's words echoed in her mind. For Claudia, safety was one thing, but to have to suffer Daniel's sharp scrutiny of her private life was something else again, something she shuddered to contemplate.

Yet here she was, rushing post-haste to a ten o'clock meeting at the hotel, as if there was no danger at all. What a way to start the week!

With a flippancy that was all pretence, she strode away from her neatly parked car at the back of Normanby Hall Hotel and, with the heady greenish scent of evergreens in her nostrils, approached the entrance. Would Daniel's mood be as dismissive as it had been when he had stormed out of Lake House on Saturday night? If so, then all problems except the emotional one of wanting someone impossible would be solved. More optimistically, would he perhaps have cooled down to the point where they could now become friends of a sort?

Less than two hours later, the thought of such an event almost made her laugh aloud. When Daniel said he had finished with her, finished was what he meant.

When she'd reached his office he had been sitting on the arm of a chair in front of the big bay window, framed between heavy velvet drapes and a billow of country-house lace that filtered the strong sunlight from outside. He looked so comfortably civilised in his white trousers and cricket sweater over a casual open-necked shirt, the colour of pale ivory, that she couldn't restrain a smile of bitter-sweet pleasure from curving her lips and bringing a shine of happiness to her eyes. Sharp as ever, Daniel registered her response at once, but his glance deliberately passed over her as he turned to one of his colleagues. It was Sally, head of the design team, and Claudia waited to be asked to take a seat as Sally smiled up at Daniel, her huge hoop ear-rings clinking with the vigour of her movements.

Just when Claudia was wondering whether to make her own way to a space at the large work-table in the window, Daniel seemed to remember she was there, and made a few perfunctory introductions.

'This is Pru, this is Ben, Sally's design assistant ... And Gary, my executive assistant, you've already met.' Before she could open her mouth to reply, Daniel went on, 'Let's start, shall we? Sally? What have you come up with?'

As she rapidly described the origins of their design ideas, Pru and Ben spread colour swatches and fabrics over the table so that soon it was a heap of colour.

'This is lovely!' exclaimed Claudia in delight, making a dive for a particular piece that caught her eye. 'I think——' But before she could let them know what she thought, Daniel had swept on as if she hadn't uttered a word.

'Yes, Sally. I certainly agree with you,' he was saying, 'but what about durability? I'd prefer it in the twelve millimetre fabric if possible.'

The discussion continued. A few moments later though, Claudia couldn't help chiming in again. 'Everything in the salon is a soft peach toned with——' But again Daniel simply ignored her, so that she left with her sentence unfinished and feeling very foolish. A tide of anger swept over her, but she bided her time until once again she only managed to utter a couple of words before Daniel interrupted.

'Pru, what do you think? The ivory or the champagne? I think we can safely discount the peach.'

'But——' Claudia began. Then she froze. She could feel the long length of Daniel's leg along her own as if by accident. The shock of physical contact momentarily checked her, and by the time she had pulled herself together Pru was carefully explaining the reasons for her own preference. Suddenly Daniel seemed to be leaning right over her shoulder, as if to scrutinise the sample she happened to be holding in her hand, and she felt his breath of her cheek, smelt the faint scent of his cologne and, when she swivelled her head to look up at him, she could almost touch the wide, amused mouth that hovered so indecently close to her own. Unable to move away without drawing attention to herself, she was compelled to withstand his delicate torture with as much composure as she could muster while every instinct was telling her to make her escape while she could. Her jaw sagged when she heard what he said next.

Turning his devastating grey gaze on her, he announced blandly, 'Of course, our views are merely theoretical. When it comes down to it, the final say rests with Mrs Gray.'

She gave him a quick glance to see if he was joking, but his face was absolutely straight. How on earth had he the nerve to say such a thing when he was blocking her at every turn?

'That's very generous of you,' she replied, unable to keep the caustic tone out of her voice.

He gave her an amused glance, but didn't bother to reply, and it was like water off a duck's back, for throughout the rest of the meeting she never managed to utter more than a couple of sentences. By the time it was drawing to a close she was seething.

'I guess that just about wraps things up for now.' Daniel rose to his feet.

Now, thought Claudia, when the others go I shall give him a piece of my mind. The arrogant, overbearing, self-opinionated *swine*!

'Thank you, Sally. That was excellently presented. I'm sure we've given Mrs Gray something to think about.'

And how! Claudia scowled inwardly, while smiling serenely around the table. She, too, rose to her feet. Then her mouth dropped open as, with a brief inaudible word to his secretary, Daniel turned abruptly and left the room before Claudia could ever make a move after him. His secretary came across to her.

'I'll show you down, Mrs Gray,' she smiled.

Claudia, silently raging, was disgorged like a piece of old refuse from the precincts of Daniel's domain.

When she got back to the salon she was in a foul temper and poured it all out to Susie at once.

'If you expect any sympathy you're out of luck,' joked Susie unfeelingly. 'You've only yourself to blame.' Then, when she noticed Claudia's expression, she softened her tone and gave Claudia an affectionate pat. 'You'll get over him. And if it's any comfort just think of the good it must be doing his ego to have someone turn him down!'

'But I'm not—I—oh, I don't know!' replied Claudia irritably.

'Anyway,' went on Susie, 'the important thing is whether you got what you wanted at the meeting.'

'It wasn't that sort of meeting,' Claudia replied at once. 'He kept cutting in—which, of course, I found damned infuriating—but when it comes down to it, if I don't like their ideas I simply sling them out. Even *he* had to acknowledge that——'

'And do you like their proposals?'

'They're brilliant. He's got a super team together.'

'Good. So what are you pulling such a long face for?'

Claudia tried to force a smile. She couldn't explain to Susie that she hated the thought of having to continue to work alongside him with this animosity between them, just as she was terrified of opening her vulnerable heart to him.

What it amounted to, she now saw clearly, was that impossible thing: she wanted to have her cake, and eat it, too. If he would give her his single-minded devotion, so long as she herself could remain for ever aloof from any deeper involvement, she would be quite happy! It had to be like that, for safety's sake, because of all that had gone before.

Yet each time they met it would be like opening her veins, a deliberate, self-inflicted wound, senseless and self-destructive, no matter how lightly she pretended to take it.

Just then the phone shrilled, making her jump.

'You left your briefcase behind,' came the familiar voice down the line. As Susie departed tactfully into an adjoining room, Claudia swore silently at her own stupidity.

'Claudia, are you there?' came the voice again, sounding concerned rather than impatient.

'Yes. I can't understand how I could be so forget-ful——' she began defensively, her tone sharpening.

'I can.' There was a significant pause.

Not daring to ask what he meant, Claudia could only grip the receiver with whitening knuckles as all sensible rejoinders fled instantly from her mind.

'It's no good like this, is it, Claudia?' came his voice again. 'I hate operating like this and neither of us is getting what we want, are we?'

She held her breath, willing him to go on, to say the words which would release her from the snares of the path she had embarked upon, but she heard a sigh when she didn't answer, and all he said was, 'I'm just leaving and haven't time to bring your case over, but I'll drop it into reception on my way down ... Unless, of course, there's anything urgent in it that you'll need today? I can always send somebody over with it.'

'I wouldn't hear of such a thing,' she replied with acerbity. 'I'll pick it up myself later after work. Why should anybody else be put to any trouble on my account?' It was her stock answer, pivotal to her sense of independence. She had lived by it, fiercely, for twelve long years.

Such independence didn't seem to go down well with Daniel, or maybe he misread it as ingratitude.

'Suit yourself,' he told her curtly, and the line went dead, leaving Claudia with the feeling that she was utterly bereft. What was the song? 'Every time you say goodbye I die a little'?

It was even worse when he didn't even bother to utter the word itself.

She let a whole week trail by before bothering to pick up her case. It had only been a stage prop for the benefit of Daniel in the first place, and she had no need of it, nor of its contents, in her ordinary day-to-day life. Daniel didn't contact her again; perhaps he'd assumed she had been along to collect the case, or perhaps he simply hadn't bothered to give the matter another thought.

Before leaving work that evening, she rang reception just to make sure that it was still there. What she hoped was that the receptionist would put her straight through to Daniel, for if she tentatively put out a friendly gesture surely this silly feud would come to an end and they could at least become friends? Anything would be better than to be cast into the cold like this. But her hopes were dashed at once, for the receptionist informed her that Mr Sinnington had been out of town for some days.

'Shropshire?' puzzled Claudia when she heard.

'At one of our other hotels,' explained the voice on the other end.

Feeling that fate was decidedly against her attempts to remedy the situation, Claudia locked up after saying goodnight to the rest of the staff, and drove the short distance out of town to the hotel.

It was late now, and the sun was already setting across the fields of ripening wheat that flanked the lane leading to it. The sky, streaked with angry red, contrasted dramatically with the lush gold of the fields. From the top of the drive the hotel looked warm and inviting, but it served only to heighten Claudia's feeling that she would always be an outsider; people responded to the sophisticated woman they saw, and not to the one she was inside. Daniel was by no means alone in making that mistake.

Feeling that the one summer, long ago, which had set her life on its particular course, was very present now, she turned in between the stone pillars guarding the entrance and began to make her way along the now familiar gravelled drive to the entrance. The air had never smelled sweeter, after a brief shower of rain, and never so poignantly reminiscent of that lost summer as now.

After she picked up her case from reception she was reluctant to leave straight away. Even though she knew Daniel was safely in another town, just to be near the place where he worked made him seem close. She wanted to wrap herself a little longer in the comfort of such a bitter-sweet emotion.

One or two guests were sitting under the glass rotunda among the leafy plants, sipping drinks, but most were still at dinner, judging from the discreet sounds of tinkling glass and silver coming from across the hall. The feeling of being sent back in time was aided by the country-house elegance of the place, fading sunlight touching gold here and there from the rich colours of the furnishings. Turning back to the receptionist behind her bank of crimson peonies, she asked, 'Would it be all right if I went up to the salon to see how things are getting on?'

'Of course, Mrs Gray. I think you'll be pleasantly surprised. The decorators finished this afternoon.'

'That's wonderful,' she murmured, pretending a lightness she did not feel. As she made her way up the stairs she could only admire Daniel's business acumen, his efficiency, speed, style. She smiled wryly to herself—was there anything she could not admire about the man? Was he perfection incarnate? Not far off—but for his fickleness and for the callousness with which he had treated her long ago, that should have had her hating him for the rest of her life.

Afraid of meeting anyone, in case she got involved in conversation and spoiled her mood, she cautiously made her way upstairs to the top of the building, then she stepped through the door into what had been merely a series of attics a few weeks ago. Now, transformed into a swishly elegant salon, it waited only for its clients to bring it to life.

Curious, she inspected the sauna room, tested the showers, lingered beside the recently completed jacuzzi. A touch of a switch brought it churning to life. Everything was waiting for the word go. Longingly she looked at the creamy waters in the marble tub, but turned away. It wouldn't do to give in to temptation— any of the staff might appear unannounced and besides, she hadn't got a towel.

Regretfully she moved back towards the door, then her flesh froze. The shape of a man was silhouetted against the dying sun that glared, blood-red, through one of the windows. Her gasp made him move out of the light and his features came into full focus, light hair blazing out, bright eyes, pale gold tan, a silver-grey business suit emphasising the long elegant shape of him, as, equally startled, he breathed her name.

She happened to be wearing a white silk blouse and calf-length white silk skirt, with lots of gold chains to highlight the translucent tones of the skin at her throat. Her face, beneath its immaculate dark bob, was strikingly made up as usual, to emphasise the deep pools of her cobalt eyes.

The silence hung between them endlessly.

At last she managed to croak, 'I thought you were in Shropshire. They told me you were ...' The hair prickled along her scalp now that fate had changed its mind and presented him face to face. She had no alternative but to go ahead and make an all-or-nothing attempt to re-establish the relationship, come what may.

'I—I wanted to talk to you,' she said with shaking voice as she forced herself to confront him, 'but—I see you're back,' she went on feebly. He didn't reply at once.

Wildly, she wondered why she had been told that story about his absence, but her unspoken question was soon answered when he told her with a weary shrug,

'I just got back.'

'From Shropshire?' she exclaimed in disbelief.

'Light aircraft. I didn't walk it!' He gave a disarmingly boyish grin. There was something bright in his glance when he told her, 'I came up here to try the jacuzzi. It's just what I need after a day like today.' He paused, and she knew what was coming next even before he spoke. In fact, he didn't speak at once. His eyes spoke for him, glinting with provoking humour as they slid to the marble tub, to her slim form, and back.

He somehow moved in front of her, holding out a hand in invitation.

'No—Daniel!' She backed off.

'I haven't asked you yet,' he teased, running a hand lightly down her arm in a soothing gesture, as if smoothing ruffled fur. It was strangely effective. He was immediately aware of the turmoil he was wreaking among her emotions.

'Now you mention it——' Again he cast a glance at the waiting tub beside them. 'Surely you won't say no?'

'Daniel, stop this!'

'You're so serious these days, Claudia. Is it out of choice, or do you lack the opportunity to enjoy life as you should?'

'I wouldn't enjoy being found in a jacuzzi with you, Daniel Sinnington,' she retorted, all solemn thoughts about establishing a casual friendship with him flying out of the window.

'Who said anything about being found? That's not

part of the package. I prefer my pleasures exclusive, anyway.'

Suddenly pulling herself together she raised her head, the light of common sense in her blue eyes. 'If you seriously think you'll persuade me to undress here and now—oh, honestly, Daniel!'

'Suit yourself,' he cut in, moving nearer. 'If you don't want to undress that's your look-out.' His hands were coming up to cup her in his arms, but in the instant before she anticipated the longed-for contact, it dawned on her what the wicked smile actually meant.

'You wouldn't dare!' she breathed, as he drew her up close against his body, then she was struggling wildly, her violent hammering at his chest quashed by the steely hold he gained over her as together, he pulling one way and she the other, they slowly began to topple towards the brink then started to fall slowly, like a film in slow motion, hitting the water with an almighty splash.

When she burst to the surface, spluttering for air, it was to meet his handsome face hovering just above her and creased by an insufferable grin. Water had slicked his blond hair flat to his head.

'I hate you, Daniel Sinnington!' she yelled at the top of her voice, not caring who heard her, and feeling the worst possible kind of fool to allow him to get her into such a mess. All her earlier bitter-sweet regrets had been destroyed in an instant. Pawing hair out of her eyes, she flung herself at him, intending, if she had the strength, to drown him, impossible as she knew it was.

'You're beyond the pale, Dan, the complete end! You're mad! I hate you more than I've ever hated anybody!' she yelled again as her white pleated skirt billowed in clouds of airborne silk around her waist. He roared with laughter at her vain attempts to push it modestly down and force him under the water at the same time.

His own suit surely ruined now, he splashed water in her face, then launched himself in a surge of foam to drag her down into the scented froth with him. The action was a killing reminder of a time long ago when, as teenagers, they had sky-larked together in the pool at his home—and what followed burst vividly into Claudia's mind with a sickening sense of *déjà vu*. It made her throat congest with more than the effects of submersion. She began to drown under a tide of recollection. Then, as if to crown it all, as he pulled her close he turned his glistening face to hers and murmured, 'Now you're thoroughly disorientated, madam, maybe you'll care to tell me all about this character Toby I've been hearing so much about. Is he the man who's standing between us?'

CHAPTER SEVEN

THEY were standing waist-deep, fully clothed, in a tub full of swirling milky water, hair plastered to their scalps, clothes soaked through, glowering at each other like two cats in a sack. At any other time Claudia would have seen the funny side and dissolved at once into peals of laughter, but now it was like some kind of surreal nightmare. She imagined being pressed remorselessly under the greeny-blue scented waters, gasping for breath, sliding down unto death, while her judge and persecutor towered wrathfully above her with the scales of justice tilting firmly in his favour.

'Claudia! Stop faking! There's no need to look at me like that!' Daniel cupped her chin in one hand, forcing her to look up into the searchlight brightness of his eyes. She flinched, unable to bear such scrutiny. 'You must have known somebody would let his name drop. Did you expect to keep him out of the picture for ever?'

Not at all smiling now, when only a moment ago he had been looking—now she thought about it—rather savagely amused, he glared down, his anger visibly increased by her inability to swallow down the lump in her throat and answer him.

She felt literally choked, with fear, with grief and with a more painful sharp-edged sorrow at the pain she had already endured. Now she would have to mete it out in equal quantities if his questions persisted. So far she had clung on to secrecy because it was the only way she could survive. If he insisted in stripping away her last protection, then the result would be something for which she could take no responsibility.

'Tell me the truth for once,' he ground out, still gripping her chin painfully in one hand. 'Is *he* the man you referred to before?'

Hesitating to admit to something that even now wasn't the literal truth—Toby could hardly be called a man at his age—she was slow to answer. Daniel's expression hardened. A groan of exasperation escaped his lips.

'Claudia, nothing can be worse between us than this deliberate subterfuge. It eats away at everything there is between us. Why won't you trust me? Damn it—what reason have you to doubt me?'

At this, Claudia could merely gape. How could he have the effrontery to stand there and ask such questions? Was he suffering from total amnesia? Or did he really believe, with all his masculine arrogance, that he was without blame? Yet she had found it in her heart to forgive him for his indifference—all she wanted from him now was a tiny acknowledgement of his own share in what had happened. The words struggled for shape on her tongue, but even while she was locked in combat with them he dragged her up against his sodden shirt and, as if he couldn't help himself, began feverishly to press his hands over her hair, cupping her head between his fingers as if to protect her from unseen dangers, then bringing his lips down on to her wet forehead, muffling the words of desire that came spilling from his lips.

'I want to kiss you to bits, you torturing little cheat,' he groaned. 'Don't you feel the honesty between us when we touch?' He shook her impatiently. 'Can't you see? How can you deny anything so plain? I've already told you I don't care who else there used to be in your life, or even who there still is—they're finished for you now, don't you understand? Stop running from what exists between us!'

Like any man, he had his standard quota of jealousy for the woman he loved, but for Claudia he could make exceptional allowances for her past, and for her present, too, if necessary. And he had enough self-confidence to feel that once she trusted him he would be able to dispose of any other opposition in a moment. But first she had to be able to talk to him about this unsatisfactory and generally absent lover of hers.

He would show her the futility of a life sacrificed to a man who cared so little for her that he would refuse her marriage and the proper abiding attention a woman such as she deserved.

'Why are you so stuck on him?' he muttered savagely. 'He's never around, as far as I can see. What hold does he have over you? Why doesn't he marry you?'

At this, her eyes widened. He imagined the shock on her face was pain, visible and profound, but he didn't care what further pain he inflicted. Her fidelity was self-destructive, an indulgence. He would strip the romantic illusions away like a doctor stripping off a plaster.

'He can care nothing for you, Claudia. So why do you go on with him? Have you no pride? No sense of your own worth?'

When, in the confusion of her thoughts, she could still find no answer, he ground on more hurtfully, as he thought aloud, 'The truth is he's probably thrown you over, but as long as you're still besotted with him he'll keep you dangling on a string. He's using you—and you know it!'

He glared into the smooth, perfect oval of her face and thought how stubborn she was—she showed no expres-

sion except perhaps puzzlement. Yet what he had just
said must have hurt. It must have—unless she had a
heart made of stone. He gave a laugh born of sheer
frustration at his inability to get through to her.

Claudia felt a twinge of guilt when she saw how his
face twisted with inner anguish at his wild, wide-of-the-
mark attempt to understand her silence. His face seemed
to blur and waver. God, now she was going to cry! He
noticed the single tear wind its way down her cheek
before she had time to dash it away.

So there was some feeling there. The fact that it must
be for another man made him mad with despair. Hold
on, he told himself. Easy now.

Noticing his changing expression, she tried to pull
away again, but despite his surge of compassion for her
he wasn't in the mood to let her go so easily. He
increased the pressure just a fraction, enough to keep her
prisoner against him.

'You can't escape this time, Claudia,' he told her, to
underline his action. 'This time I'm going to make you
face the truth. Even if you can't love me—you're going
to stop living for a man who doesn't care a damn for you.
You're worth more than that!'

'Don't—it's—it's not like that,' Claudia at last
managed to stutter. 'I know what I'm doing, Daniel.
Please believe me!' She paused, moved by his emotion,
not doubting at this moment that he felt something
powerful for her, but doubting its ability to last because
of the way he had once been, and doubting, too, its
survival power when he knew the truth behind her
reticence.

'It's not like that, you say? Then tell me how it is.
Why are you never together?' he persisted.

'He's—he's doing other things,' she stammered,

trying again to struggle free.

'Keep still. I haven't finished yet. Tell me, is it something like habit that keeps you faithful?'

'No—of course not!' she exclaimed.

'What is it, then? Lust, love—money?' he continued before she could say anything else. His eyes were fastened on her expression, as if trying to gauge every nuance of her reaction. 'Is that it? Money?' he asked in astonishment, his grip slackening not one bit, although something else seemed to change. It made her shiver, and she tried to smile at the absurdity of what he was saying, but his remorseless probing seemed to fix her smile artificially and a blush began to burn unaccountably. Her embarrassment seemed to confirm her guilt. She was feeling guilty because she was looking guilty!

'You're crazy!' she muttered. A wavering sense of unreality blurred the outlines of his face again. This can't be happening, she thought feverishly, he's holding me in the water as if he'll never let me go, and me, I'm blushing as if I'm guilty of this last monstrous distortion!

Suddenly all she wanted was to get out, away from the sexuality of his warm, wet body with its touching and parting and touching again, as the swaying waters bubbled and churned around them.

Her skirt was undulating around her waist, leaving her legs bare and ultra-sensitive to the pressure of his strong-boned frame as it brushed lightly against her. The seductive massage of the waves fingered her body to a state of relaxation that made it hyper-sensitive to the pressure of his touch. Her limbs seemed to float with a strange weightlessness that enhanced the dreamlike sensation, and their two bodies became entwined by the sinuous curvings of the water being forced from the jets.

Daniel's face seemed pale. 'He's the one who finances your business, your expensive tastes,' he stated flatly through scarcely parted lips. 'That's why the secrecy . . . that explains everything.'

'There's no need to look at me as if I've just crawled from under a stone!' She strove to keep the tremor out of her voice. 'What else do married women do but live off their men——' She made her eyes hard. 'Are you saying that's any more honest than what I do?'

The red herring made his jaw tighten visibly and his lips compress into an unforgiving line. Then the expression in his eyes softened, turning them from Atlantic-grey to the gentler grey of doves' feathers.

'Darling Claudia! You'll have to do better than that! I simply don't believe you! Nobody changes as much as that!'

'What do you mean?' she demanded, confused by his about-turn.

'Do you imagine I've forgotten your shame at all those scrapes you got yourself into when you were seventeen?'

She looked at him blankly, waiting for him to go on.

'You tried to act like a hard little rebel—just as you are now—but you forget one thing, I was the one who played father confessor to you. I knew all your secrets, didn't I? And I learned what made you tick.'

'So?' she managed to utter.

'So—you would never do anything that compromised you, living off a man like some cheap whore.' He became thoughtful then, as if a new idea had suddenly struck him, and murmured, as if half to himself, 'Yes, you were a tough little customer in your way. Damned independent with it. You'd never beg a penny from anybody, not if you were on the verge of starvation. In fact, you would rather die than ask anybody for help in anything. Don't think I've forgotten that . . .'

'Everybody changes,' she muttered thickly, only wanting to escape the brunt of further speculation.

'Not to that extent.'

This sudden declaration of his belief in her was undermining—it made it difficult to brazen out the situation. Angry with herself for weakening, she tried to fight it by struggling out of his grasp, shouting hoarsely, 'Let me go, will you, Daniel? This has gone on long enough!'

To her surprise and relief, braced as she was for a struggle, he let her go at once, with a knowing smile on his face that seemed to bode no good for her peace of mind at all.

He mocked, 'What? Going back to him, are you?'

'Like this?' She scowled, playing his game, and looking down at her ruined clothes as if her appearance was all that counted.

'I'll get them dried for you. But you'll have to come up to my suite.'

Noticing her startled expression, he added, 'Unless of course you'd prefer to drive back in that state.'

'I would if it wouldn't attract attention,' she muttered.

'Anything rather than get too close to me? What are you afraid of, Claudia? Sex in general, or just me?'

'In view of what you were trying to imply earlier,' she sparked back, 'I would have thought you'd guess the reason—it's because the price isn't right.'

His eyes momentarily clouded, but she could see the visible quenching of the automatic response. He gave a soft laugh. 'Name your price, baby. You may get a pleasant surprise!' He chuckled maliciously, adding,

'I'm willing to outbid any rival you care to name. Try me—if you dare!'

'You . . .' She nearly brought a hand up to smash across his face, then she noticed the silver glint in his eyes, and realised he was trying to take a rise out of her again.

'Some hope, Daniel Sinnington. I'd rather die than give in to you for any price!' Claudia began to wade towards the edge of the pool, but was hampered by the billowing folds of her skirt. Daniel followed, easily outstripping her, so that by the time she reached the edge he was barring the way. She knew what was coming before it even happened, but imagined right until the last second that she could keep the situation under control long enough to make her escape.

What she feared was that there would be no question of fighting back. And it was justified. As his arms looped round her waist to drag her body up against his own, her desire to surrender to him engulfed her reason.

As if to confirm her total capitulation, a phrase began to hammer through her mind, a phrase she dared not utter, a phrase of surrender which, once spoken aloud, would have betrayed her heart completely. It echoed again and again, I love you Daniel, I can't resist you, don't hurt me, Daniel. Please don't hurt me. I love you.

The only token of this silent litany was the small sigh that escaped her parted lips as his own came down to ravage softly over her own.

There was something bitter-sweet in her surrender, knowing that it brought them close to the inevitable ending. Sweet torture, she cried inwardly, worth it, worth it for you, Daniel, my only love. Then his beloved mouth slid provokingly over her damp face and down the side of her neck to her collarbone, where it made a detour into the soft hollow of her throat, while all the time his fingers pulled at the buttons of her silk blouse, sliding under the taut lace of her camisole as soon as they found a way, to seek refuge around the smooth mounds of her breasts. She felt the silk inch from off her shoulders and go floating away as he released it completely, then his other hand snaked beneath the constricting lace that remained, dragging up to reveal her naked breasts to his sight.

With a stifled groan he dipped his head to them, the waters swirling in a frenzy of perfumed bubbles to cover his face and she saw, through half-parted lids, his blond hair darken as water jetted over it. Allowing her eyes to close completely, she began to sink back under his weight, cushioned on the powerful jets that made their bodies weightless, and lifted by his hands as they slid round her hips to bring her close beneath him.

Then her own hands were slithering inside his blue shirt, her drooping lids momentarily opening to delight in the flash of bronze with its spray of blond hair bright against the darker tone of his skin. With a thrust of his broad shoulders, his shirt followed her blouse on the frothing waves. One hand came down, welding her pelvis to his own as they undulated amid the foam like a single sea plant in the depths of a tropical ocean. For a length of time that seemed suspended they shared the experience of floating in a half-world of rushing blue water with the light glinting off it.

He knew he had stormed the rampart she had built against him by the way she offered no resistance to his exploration of her fluid curves, and he marvelled at how suddenly she had yielded to his caresses, laying her cheek trustingly against his, lips partly open, blue eyes blurry with desire.

Claudia was full of wonder that his touch could still drain her will to resist, and the glance he lingered over her face mesmerised her, out-flanking the arguments of logic and common sense, leaving her with an aching desire to have all of him, whatever dark future lay ahead. It was a reprise of the past and now, even knowing the consequences, she knew she would suffer it all again— anything to know the ecstasy of being in his arms once more.

Her residual anger against him for the pain he had caused long ago had evaporated at the moment of their first kiss. It left her with a new sense of freedom that enabled her to give herself in all the honesty of her love.

Joying in the strength that bore her through the water, she allowed him to lead her to the marble steps that led up from the pool. The weight of their sodden clothes seemed to pull them both back into its embrace. She stumbled in bare feet, her shoes having long since disappeared, and, reaching out for his support, allowed him to give her the protection she yearned for. Gently he forced her to slide down on to the warm marble at the edge of the pool. His desire flamed through him, stimulating her own so that she abandoned herself to his touch without shame. Every rippling movement of his body along her own received an answering response from hers and, released from habitual restraint, she bent her head to return his feverish kisses, allowing her lips to find their own way over the firm, golden muscles, trailing wantonly down over his flat stomach, making him gasp with pleasure as she echoed the touch of his lips on her body with these explorations of her own. Biting and licking every vibrant inch of him, she mingled her moans of ecstasy with his until their desire reached fever pitch. Their bodies slid together like two halves of one being, achieving completion at last in a final mingled cry of triumph.

Shuddering with the convulsions of receding ecstasy, Claudia knew again the frighteningly vulnerable state to which he could bring her. Eyes suddenly flickering wide open, they met his, seeking reassurance from the liquid silverlight in them. He held her close, shuddering too in the aftermath of passion, and reassuring her with his kisses.

As their recovery slowly brought the outside world into focus he began to raise her from the damp tiles, rubbing her chilled skin until she sat up as if waking from a deep dream.

'There's my robe over there,' he told her huskily. 'Slip it on while I rescue the rest of your stuff.'

As she picked up her skirt from the poolside where it had been dropped, she saw him dive under the water and come back up a few seconds later, holding her silk blouse and a shoe. With his straight blond hair slicked down over his forehead and the smile he flashed her, he reminded her of the boy she had first loved. First love, only love, she told herself with a strange, satisfying air of finality.

Unaware of the way her thoughts were ranging, he brought the rescued items from the pool to lay them like trophies at her feet. His laughter-filled eyes flicked over her naked form, changing instantly to another mood and, recognising it, Claudia tugged the belt tightly round her waist, modestly concealing herself inside the long white towelling robe, dwarfed by it, and caressed by its softness like a momentary, more innocent substitute for the touch of the man she loved.

Daniel laughed as she averted her glance when he strode naked and bronzed from the water, revelling in

his male splendour with an air of such naturalness that
she was ashamed of her own momentary prudishness. It
had been a long time since she had been in such intimate
circumstances with a man. It was an almost new
experience. As if to spare her blushes, he wrapped an
almost inadequately small red towel round his waist,
which only served to draw attention to what he was
pretending to conceal.

Then, as they moved towards the door leading to the
harsher reality of the outside world, he stayed her for a
moment within the protecting circle of his arms.

'Tell me in words, so I know it's true, Claudia—he
means less than nothing to you. Tell me, darling. Your
body says it's true. Your eyes tell me. But I must hear it
from your beautiful lips.'

She noticed a brief flicker of insecurity cross his
strong, disciplined features, heard the unexpected note
of doubt in a voice that was more often resonant with the
timbre of authority and decision, before she deflected it
by quickly kissing him on the cheek, saying huskily, 'I
love you, Daniel. I always have.' She paused, and added,
'I'm afraid I always shall.'

A hesitation in his returning hug betrayed a brief flare
of suspicion at the way in which she had changed the
form of his words. He was too astute not to realise its
significance. For a moment she thought he was going to
pursue the matter—his grey eyes flashed with momentary aggression—but he settled for the gentler course,
merely telling her, 'Let's go up to my suite and have a
drink while our clothes dry off.'

He lived at the top of the west wing and it was a suite
done out in some style, like the rest of the house—but
there were added touches that gave the flowery country-
house patterns a more masculine edge. A Chinese screen,

gold flowers stitched on to black silk, stood beside an ebony marble fireplace, and the deep leather chester-fields were in strong black hide, their austerity softened by a scattering of white and grey silk tapestry cushions. A pale goat-hair rug was flung over the highly polished black woodblock floor, and the walls gleamed with the subtle sheen of pale grey silk.

'I love your view, as well,' offered Claudia enigmatically, after smiling with pleasure at the stylish elegance of his private rooms, apt expression of such a man. She moved towards the large curving bay that gave a view to the front of the Hall. It was an intense kind of pleasure to sit in the windowseat and watch him through the open door as he tossed their clothes busily into the dryer in his immaculate white and grey Italian-style kitchen. It was a bachelor apartment, impossible to envisage with the haphazard disorder of children spoiling the careful colour scheme and mirrored, finger-markable surfaces, she thought, as she looked around.

'It suffices for the time being,' he said, coming through into the living-room, still wearing only the scarlet towel round his waist. She tried to ignore the quiver of desire that fluttered through her body at the sight of such a perfectly muscled torso, his long, well-shaped legs tapering to firm, elegantly formed feet. He crossed the wool rug and came to a stop in front of her, looking down, a pensive smile on his face at the sound of her cool formality of tone. It scarcely matched her appearance—dishevelled locks hanging wetly to her shoulders—or her attire—despite the neat protective bow in which she had tied the belt.

'The view, I mean. It suffices. For inspiration, should I need it.' He referred to the geometry of green fields outside the window. He was transfixed by her face, its beauty, its oval perfection, and its innocent, scrubbed look, now that the make-up had been washed off during their aquatic incident.

'The suite, too,' he went on, only giving half his attention to what he was saying. 'I sleep here. That's all I need it for.'

She raised cobalt eyes a fraction, and looked at him through lash-veiled eyes, as if to dwell fully on the contours of his physique would invite disaster.

'Is it home?' she considered gravely, raising her eyes to his quickly, skidding over the danger of letting them rest on his near nakedness.

'I used to think it was—until recently.' His smile twisted into a rueful grimace. She understood at once what he was trying to tell her, but read it as casual flattery—the coinage of the seductive art. She didn't need it, shame to say. Her answering smile told him what was in her mind and he hastened to explain.

'I've started to wonder why it is I've never wanted a home, family . . .'

'And why don't you?' She eyed him levelly.

'Till now it's been the easy course. It was easy to make a god of ambition. People happened to like what I did. I suppose so long as they go on making my hotels a success, I'll go on trying to find more ways to please them——' He spread his hands. 'Maybe I'll slow down when I'm forty. Retire, perhaps. Buy a pretty house somewhere. Acquire a wife along the way, and settle down to raise a family.'

'You? Settle down?' Claudia laughed despite herself, taking his plans as idle pipe-dreams.

'First the wife, perhaps?' He slanted a smile towards her upturned face and, in the same throwaway tone, murmured, 'Don't look at me like that. I'll drown in your eyes.'

Before she could deflect him he lowered his head to graze her lips with his own, then still in the same movement curved away from her, calling over his shoulder as he crossed the room, 'Coffee will be ready soon. I'll just——' he paused at the bedroom door. '——slip into something less comfortable!'

With a flash of white teeth that stormed her heart, he disappeared into one of the rooms off the main one, but as he opened and closed cupboards he continued to send fragments of conversation out to her.

'We've managed to side-track ourselves again, Claudia . . .' There was a pause, the sound of a drawer closing. 'How do we always manage to get off the point?' A cupboard door slammed.

Her imagination spun tantalising images of his state of undress. The sound of a zip added vividly to her suppositions.

'Or do you think that what seems off the point is in fact the real point of our relationship?' He came to the door.

Her imagination had failed to prepare her for the reality. Thigh-hugging white trousers gripped his muscular form so that his unclothed torso gleamed with the mellowness of stripped pinewood by contrast. As he spoke he was pulling a sweater over his head. Its french blue contrasted vibrantly with the blond, as yet uncombed, hair. Even with it sticking up awry, he was devastating. His eyes crinkled at the corners as he smiled across the room at her. He's so blond and heroic. Like a space captain, she thought whimsically. Guide me to the stars! She smiled at the sweater he was pulling into place—with its red and white hoops round the sleeves, it was the sort of thing Toby might wear. She tried to joke, to hide how moved she felt.

'What's the matter?' He came to stand over her again, running his fingers through his damp hair, his teeth making a brief dazzle against the darker tone of his skin.

'You look so——' Her cobalt eyes veiled. Memory flooded back, engulfing her sense, constricting her throat with grief for what might have been. The futility of regret added to her distress.

'Don't cry!' Daniel was at once beside her, cradling her in his arms, stifling her incipient tears with little kisses in the hollows of her eyes, pressing his lips randomly over her neck, her hair, her face.

'Don't ever cry again. That's an order,' he murmured, alarmed at the brittleness of her façade, the ease with which it could be pierced. 'Why are you crying? Are you thinking about him? Are you frightened to tell him about us? Don't be. The future is for us, Claudia. You can't run away from it. If he loves you at all, he'll want your happiness.'

Her eyes flickered open beneath his lips. 'It's not that, Daniel, believe me. It's—it's you . . . you looked so . . . it reminded me of the past when . . . I was so in love with you—and——' How to explain that love betrayed was a deep wound, sometimes impossible to heal completely? However often the pain was salved, the original wound would break out in all its former agony.

'I never really knew——' he murmured against the side of her face. 'At least, I thought I did. I believed we were both equally crazily in love with each other . . . then you left. No word.'

His arms strengthened around her, as if now he would hold on to her for ever.

'I often wondered why you did that. I must have

meant very little for you to give me the boot so quickly.
It made no sense. Eventually I arrived at the conclusion
that it all came down to girlish pique, because I'd gone
away on holiday, sending only postcards. It seems so
long ago now, but at the time you inflicted hell on me—
not to say battered my poor ego!'

'*Your* ego?' She dared a kiss on the side of his jaw,
darting her tongue in little fluttering trails to the corner
of his mouth. 'And it wasn't the postcards——' She held
back just as his mouth opened to take hers. 'I got the
postcards, Dan. All twenty of them, and all on the same
day.'

'I thought they'd got lost. I wanted to sue the postal
authorities for emotional cruelty—causing a rift
between me and my beloved. Instead I played hookey
from school, hitched a lift to the aunt in Barnstaple—or
was it Dunstable?—and demanded to know your
whereabouts——'

'Wait a minute——' Claudia began to shake all over,
her image of the past beginning to crack into a
shimmering haze of misconception.

Was it wrong, this belief she had held on to? And she
had based her life upon it . . .

'Tell me slowly,' she whispered, scarlet fingernails
digging convulsively into his arm, 'tell me, Dan . . . Are
you trying to say you never got my letter?'

'Letter? What letter?' The puzzlement on his face
gave her the answer as clearly as his bewildered
repetition of her words.

'I wrote to you when I left Holcomb,' she told him
rapidly. 'When you didn't reply, I thought——' Her
face broke into a thousand pieces, each one an image of
grief as the waste of heartache stretched unending
around her. The years, days, minutes of grieving for

him, hating him, finally coming to terms with loving him in vain, burned through her body like a fire-storm, leaving a desolation behind it that made her speechless.

'You thought it had been a casual fling for me?' he questioned, eyes full of tender astonishment. 'Oh, darling Claudia, my precious, how could you think ... Do you know what I did? What I went through? I felt crazy when I discovered you'd left without leaving any address. I raged against all girls, with names I didn't know I knew, cursed the sense of duty that made me go with my family to Italy for a whole month—I thought it would never end. I counted the seconds, literally. Then, when I came back—nothing! You'd simply vanished.'

The reason for that burned again with the old sense of shame that had forced her to such secrecy.

'I didn't know how to face it. Eventually I forced myself to sit down and think it out. The psychology of girls seemed beyond me—but I half thought you were angry because I'd paid more attention to keeping the balance at home than to you ...' He squeezed her shoulders. 'You had a rough time that summer. I felt like a heel for leaving you when you needed me, but at that age one tends to do as one's parents request. Some of the time, anyway ...'

'I needed you, Daniel——' She stopped, struck by a sudden realisation. If he had never got her letter—he could never have known just how much she had needed him that autumn. He called it a rough time. How rough he could not know, even now.

'My love,' he went on, hugging her protectively, though tragically too late. 'I managed to get the aunt's address out of someone,' he went on, 'but by the time I tracked her down you'd moved on. I can't understand why you didn't leave your new address with her. Did you have a row? Walk out? Or were you trying to cover your tracks for some reason?'

Claudia flinched at the accidental accuracy of this last question and said hurriedly, 'She wasn't my real aunt. I think she was one of dad's ex-girlfriends from way back.'

'They gave me short-shrift anyway, she and her husband,' he continued. 'I'd believed I could charm her into telling me where you were. But her old man wasn't at all susceptible to boyish charm. He told me to clear off in no uncertain manner.'

'It's understandable—my being the daughter of his wife's ex-lover. I didn't stay long. I was so obviously unwelcome.' Yes, there had been that, on top of her growing panic.

'But where on earth did you go to? You told me you had no other relations. I didn't know where else to look for you. You seemed to vanish into thin air.'

'Where do all young girls go? I went to live on the streets paved with gold. I went to London.' She tried to make light of it. Lies, despite everything, never came easily. To lie to Daniel now, when they were so close and his eyes were filled with such trust and love for her, was abhorrent, so she tried to imply that it was the bright lights that had lured her away. The truth seemed too big, too ugly, to let loose among the fragile shoots of this tender regrowth of love. She was overwhelmed by the possible consequences, and feared it would be too much to blurt out without careful preparation of the ground. When he learned the truth and decided to leave her, she could not survive a second bereavement. It was fear of the consequences that still held her tongue in check, thwarting her natural honesty.

'London!' he exclaimed. 'It would have had me haunting the place if I'd know!' He gave a grimace.

'After being seen off the premises at Dunstable I eventually went back to school. Remember I was in the upper sixth? Well, I though that was that—the end of a beautiful affair.' His expression was rueful. 'I guess the whole thing made me grow up fast. There were long talks with matron. She tried to tell me girls were like that. Fickle. Never knowing from one day to the next what they really wanted. It took me years to realise it was only a half-truth——' He grinned briefly in a way which made her heart stop. 'I think I'll go back and tell her she was wrong. She wouldn't believe me when I said you were the exception. "She must be some sort of angelic paragon," she told me. I said you were . . .'

He trailed a thoughtful kiss over her hair. 'I always knew that's what you were, even when I was most angry with you. My angelic paragon!'

Claudia's sharp laugh, humourless and distancing, made him recoil as abruptly as if she had hit out at him. He tilted her face up to his, and their eyes locked.

'But that's how I think of you,' he insisted. 'Don't you believe me?' His eyes searched her face for doubts. 'Do you think I'm lying to you?'

'No,' she muttered, struggling to make sense of her reaction. 'It's—it's so far from the truth . . . Daniel, I'm not the person you think I am——'

'Let me be the judge of that.' He grazed her lips with his own, in a series of little caresses. 'Why put yourself down all the time?' He bestowed another little burst of kissing all over her face. 'Somebody seems to have caused a monster-sized dent in your ego at some time,' he concluded.

If only he knew, she thought despairingly.

He tracked kisses over her hair, and when he came to look into her eyes his own were thoughtful. Leaning down to breathe into her ear, he whispered, 'Let me have the job of reinflating it—I've room for a giant ego in my life!'

'As well as your own?' she tried to quip, controlling the tremor in her voice with an effort.

'As a complement to my own—so I don't get unmanageably conceited.'

'You're playing again,' she gibed.

'Not completely.' Grey eyes darkened to an oceanic hue. 'I don't know why you doubt me. You seem to have everything going for you, yet there's still something, some reticence, some mystery . . .' He paused. 'I refuse to be fazed by anything—you can tell me anything, Claudia. You can trust me. You must know that——'

His warmth lapped around her, coaxing the truth bit by bit from its hiding place to the fore-front of her mind. The desire to give herself entirely into his hands was sweeping her along. Was this the moment she had been waiting for? Could she really trust him to the extent he suggested? How she wanted to spill out everything within her heart and if anyone should know the truth it would have to be Daniel. Daniel, her love.

Holding her breath until it hurt, she began to speak in a voice that was little more than a whisper.

'Daniel—there is something. I thought I'd resolved it long ago. But ever since we met up again it's been preying on my mind . . . I suppose I've always known I would have to tell you some day . . .'

At first she didn't register what the noise beside her was, but when it eventually penetrated her consciousness, she stopped talking instantly, suddenly terrified of the world she had been about to open up.

'I won't answer it, go on,' he told her, grey eyes holding hers as her cheeks flamed with fiery colour. She began to shake with fear at how close she had edged towards self-betrayal. The clamour persisted, bringing intimations of the world outside to their cocoon of newly ripening trust, tearing it to ribbons. Reality burst in. The moment was lost.

She lifted her head. 'Answer it,' she begged. 'It may be important.'

Loath to part from her for an instant, he stretched out a hand to pull the phone from under the cushion on the floor beside her.

'Yes?' He paused long enough for her to notice how his eyes darted towards her, and his whole body tensed.

'She's here,' he clipped. Without a word he handed the phone to her.

'But how—who knows I'm here?' she asked.

'My receptionist's an intuitive woman,' he remarked, without looking at her.

Alerted by his manner, her eyes were fastened on him as if to gleam every nuance of meaning from his expression as she spoke into the mouthpiece. 'Yes?' she queried with a frown.

'Mrs Hampshire?' came a voice, at first unrecognisable, then, as its identity took shape, her face paled. 'Yes, yes, where is he now?' She gripped the phone with suddenly whitening knuckles. 'Hospital! Yes, yes—which one?'

A pause. Daniel marvelled at the translucent pallor that instantly covered her skin. Such feeling, such compassion, instant, honest, direct—the recipient was a lucky fellow. Tactfully, feeling a weight tighten like a steel brace across his shoulders, he found his way into the kitchen where the forgotten coffee was bubbling in the pot. He listened as she put the phone down on the black marble coffee-table—it had always reminded him of a memorial slab, he thought irrelevantly as he raised his head to watch her come to stand at the kitchen door.

Gone was the lacquered model-girl image, gone too was the sweet, vulnerable once-seventeen-year-old, lovable and funny in the ridiculously over-sized bathrobe. Here was another Claudia—older, panicky, peremptory, face ashen, blue eyes like a blind girl, oblivious to the anguish she was causing.

'Get my clothes, Daniel. I have to go.'

'Why?' His question was flat, as unemotional as his expression.

'You heard. There's been a accident. I'm needed at the hospital.'

He didn't ask who was involved. He didn't need to. Her reaction of total concern was enough. She was broken up by fear. He countered her request, anything to keep her with him and damn this most important person in her life. What right had he to exist? Especially now, after this evening.

'Your clothes are wet.'

'I don't care!' Her voice broke with the strain. She was almost shouting. 'I'll wear them wet!' In her distress, she ran to the dryer and tried to stop it.

'No. Like this.' He pressed the switch. 'You have to wait three minutes.'

'I can't!'

'Three minutes? It won't open otherwise.' Then compassion for her swamped his mind and heart. What did his petty desire mean beside this engulfing despair? She looked crazed with anxiety. And he had thought it was just a played-out affair, meaning nothing to her. What had he done to her already this evening through his animal behaviour?

'Here——' He poured a cup of coffee. 'Drink it while you wait.'

'I can't.'

'Do try please. It'll help.'

'Oh, Daniel!' She was relieved to have him tell her what to do. Her own thoughts whizzed like out of control carriages on a big dipper, fed by the energy of her worst imaginings.

'It's Toby,' she blurted between sips of the black coffee he offered. 'He's been in some sort of accident. They seem to know nothing. Those fools at the hospital!' She took another sip, put down the cup and looked at him with eyes that seemed to see nothing of the man in front of her, wearing his palpable concern like a hair shirt.

'I don't trust officials. They say they know nothing. But perhaps they do. It's—what if . . .? Oh God, get my clothes! Please—I must go!'

Like a robot, stripped of all feeling save the conventional manifestations of concern programmed into him, Daniel snapped open the door of the dryer, shook out her clothes, noted that they were dry enough to put on, and handed them to her without speaking. The seductive slipping away of his bathrobe down the curving length of her honey-cream skin, to which he had looked forward with unashamed hunger, took place in an instant, here in the kitchen and with as much clinical detachment as if a procedure in the hospital she was hurrying to reach. When she got to the outer door he had to let her go, all offers to drive her over to the hospital being rejected with a dismissive shake of the head.

'I'll need the car.' For what, she didn't specify. It seemed useless to argue with her.

'I'll drive you there and get a taxi back after dropping you off.'

'No!' She began to back through the door, one hand already fumbling for her car-keys.

He felt he should insist, should protect her from what it was that lay in wait for her, but how would it be, after the intimacy they had just shared, to try to hold her hand even in sympathy, not lust, beside the bed of the man who was still her lover? He had no right to inflict such a conflict of loyalties upon her.

There was a blind look in her eyes, and she moved like one deaf to anything but the alarm bells in her own head. Reluctantly he knew he would have to let her face this one by herself.

Before the door closed—negating their recent intimacy—he heard himself say, 'I hope it's not as bad as you think.'

And after the door had closed behind her he wondered what art of self-negation had prevented the words from sticking in his throat.

Spurning the pot of fresh black coffee, he poured himself something stronger and drank it rapidly while he stood looking out at the green patchwork of fields that stretched impassively to the horizon.

'Daniel Sinnington, not fazed by anything,' he thought mockingly, '... except this lovely, haunted, destroying woman, Claudia ... Claudia ...'

CHAPTER EIGHT

TWENTY minutes later, Claudia was skidding recklessly into the hospital car park. Since she had donned her own clothes again she had been conscious of a dampness over her back and along her arms, and put it down to the fact that she had snatched her clothes out of Daniel's dryer prematurely, but when she spun the steering wheel the slipperiness of her hands on the leather rim brought another cause to mind.

'Keep calm, keep calm, keep calm!' she admonished in anything but a calm manner as she jammed the car into the first vacant place she came across. Almost at a run, she wound through endless rows of cars until she came to the main entrance. The hospital, all its lights blazing in the dusk, was like a huge liner at anchor. Did it bear a cargo of despair? she wondered as she clicked across the patio to the automatic plate-glass doors and on towards the long reception desk where she stood fuming with impatience until her turn came up.

'Childrens' Ward Ten,' the receptionist told her. 'Please speak to Matron.'

With a heart thudding like a jack hammer, she found a lift and negotiated what seemed like miles of impersonal corridor until she came to an isolated desk in a sea of space, and the ward number she wanted. Before she could begin to look round for Matron, a lanky bundle of energy came hurtling from a bed half hidden behind a green curtained screen aslant the entrance to the ward.

'Toby!' Convulsively she grabbed him to her in a bearhug of relief at seeing him not only conscious, but alive and kicking too. Then she held him more gently, remembering he was supposed to be hurt.

130

'What's the matter, darling? I thought you'd be flat in bed at least,' she demanded, searching his face sharply for some sign of injury.

'I'm fine,' he announced, looking rather sheepish.

'Then what are you doing in here?' she demanded.

'They insisted. At school.'

'Whatever for?'

'Nothing, really.'

'Toby! Now I want the truth! I've been out of my mind with worry.' Fleetingly she recalled Daniel's expression as she had taken the call. If it had scared her, it had certainly given him pause for thought, at least, her reaction had done. She must put that right as soon as possible.

'Toby?' she demanded now, all mother. 'What happened?'

'Well,' he began reluctantly. 'You know it was the fourth form picnic today?'

'How could I ever forget?' Even as she put on a stern face she was still searching his strong young body for signs of injury. It would be like Toby to play down a broken leg or something. She glanced at the firm legs, silently registering the scuffed knees, drooping socks, and new, but ancient-looking sneakers. OK in the leg department, she registered. He was looking sheepish again, so she gave him a little shake. 'So?' she prompted.

'Somebody fell in the river, the idiot.'

'Not you?'

'Not me.'

'So—so what?' she queried. 'They can all swim, can't they?'

'Well—we happened to be at Aysgarth Falls.'

'Ah, so that was the mystery trip——' she began, then she stared. 'You mean they fell *into* the Falls? Is he all right now?'

'I guess so.'

'You're sure? You sound doubtful.'

'It was Pugsie,' he admitted grudgingly. 'He's in the bed over there.'

Claudia shot a glance across the half-darkness of the ward, where a silent mound suggested the presence of Toby's best friend Julian Cairn. Pug? Cairn? She supposed there was a kind of lateral logic to it. 'Why isn't he careering about the ward like you?' she demanded suspiciously.

'He cracked his head on a bit of a rock, and they thought he had concussion. He's asleep now. We've just had supper. It was terrific. Chips and rice with skin on.'

'Sounds delicious. And you're sure you're all right?'

'They said I could go if you came to pick me up.'

'Wait a minute. If it was Ju—Pugsie who fell in—why are you here?'

Beginning to relax, Toby now looked caught for a moment and became rather interested in the retying of his shoelace. 'I told you. It was school. You know what they're like. They thought I needed checking out.'

Claudia refrained from comment, and at that moment, lifting her head, caught sight of a pleasant-looking nurse smiling at her through the window of a small office on the other side of the corridor. She came out to greet Claudia at once.

'You his mum? He's ready for home and bed, I should think. Don't they bother to feed him the rest of the year?' she asked, giving him a beaming smile.

Claudia returned it. 'For your caterer's sake, I'm glad he's not in for long. By the way,' she paused, 'why was he brought in? He looks the same as usual to me.'

'Ah well, we had to be sure there were no internal injuries. And he was a little dazed too, to start with.'

'I'm surprised that was noticed.' Dazed herself, but with nothing worse than relief, Claudia helped Toby gather his things together.

The matron gave them a smile of farewell, saying, 'A

little rest, perhaps, and then he can go straight back to school.'

Outside Claudia turned on him with a withering expression. 'Honestly, Toby, trust you and Julian to go and fall in. Was Mr Cuthbert mad at you?'

'He was OK.'

'Did he have to drive you in to the hospital himself? It must have brought the picnic to an abrupt end.'

'No. They sent an ambulance. It was great. They put their lights on.'

'That's terrible, Toby. Ambulance men are busy enough, without having to go driving from one side of the country to the other because of a couple of silly boys.'

Suddenly all the pent-up emotion of the last few hours exploded to the surface. The moment with Daniel, so delicately approached and now in all probability never to be repeated, wrenched her emotions out of joint, making her turn to Toby with a spurt of unaccustomed anger.

'At your age, Toby, you should show more common sense than to play around on the edge of a dangerous waterfall. What if you'd been swept among the rocks? You'd have been drowned for sure.'

'We *were* swept among the rocks, and we weren't drowned——'

'Then you can count yourself extremely lucky! It's the sort of behaviour I would expect from a six-year-old, not a——'

'We weren't playing, mum,' Toby broke in vehemently. 'We were trying to rescue a small calf that was stuck in the reeds on the edge of the bank.'

'That's no excuse,' she repeated. Relief at finding him safe and sound mollified her anger somewhat, and she gave him a tight hug when they got to the car.

'I don't think I can take a scaring like that very often,' she told him, and was pleased to hear him promise to be more careful in future, even though she knew it was a promise that would be forgotten by morning.

'Better come back to the flat for the night,' she told him as they drove out of the hospital grounds. 'It's hardly worth going over to Lake House at this time of night, and I don't suppose they're expecting you back at school at this time, are they?'

'No. I told them I'd stay with you.'

'I wonder you dare show your face at school after this. You'd better go and apologise to Mr Cuthbert first thing in the morning.'

Settling him safely into bed in his little room at the flat, she breathed a sigh of relief as soon as she had kissed him goodnight and closed the door. Now that she could relax, she could see things in a clearer perspective and her wild panic of earlier in the evening seemed absurd. Yet the official voice on the other end of the line, because it had been able to tell her so little, had laid the seed-bed for what were not totally irrational fears. Mothers the world over would understand what she had gone through.

Now all she had to do was ring Daniel and explain. If she had reached the point of confessing that Toby was her son, not her lover, and been thwarted through no fault of her own, now must surely be the time to rectify matters. She would shut her eyes to the consequences. Things would have to take their own course after this. At the very least, she owed an apology to him for dashing off like a mad thing with no explanation. Shouting at him like that! Demanding her clothes back as if he was a laundryman! His vaguely recollected offer of help brought a smile to her face. How sweet he was! Even when she behaved so badly, his good nature wasn't disturbed. How could she not love such a good man?

Kicking off her court shoes, she settled down in an armchair and drew the phone towards her. She would invite him over for a drink, if he didn't think it too late. It would be better to tell him to his face why she had

gone dashing off like that—to break it to him gently that
she had a son. The presence of Toby in the flat now
would prevent the situation becoming unmanageable.
The thought made her wrinkle her brow. She had never
felt so out of her depth with anyone.

It was as if Daniel only had to say to her, 'Yes, yes . . .
come to me . . .' and she could find no strength to resist.
It was like being seventeen all over again—except that
this time, surely she had learned her lesson?

Dialling his number, she waited impatiently for him
to answer. When there was no reply, she waited ten
minutes, then dialled again. Still out of luck, she flicked
open a book, but flung it aside after a few minutes and
reached once more for the phone. It was midnight when
she decided to try reception. The night porter seemed
unsurprised at her request to speak to Mr Sinnington.
Obviously, she thought tartly, his countless girlfriends
call him at all hours.

'I'm afraid Mr Sinnington left the hotel about eight
o'clock and hasn't yet returned,' came the smooth reply.
'May I take a message, madam?'

'Er—no—no, it's all right,' she faltered. 'I'll try
tomorrow.'

With a deadening of emotion, she cut off her line to
the hotel. Of course he has girlfriends, she told herself
fiercely. How could a man like that not have? She had
read it for herself in the Press, too. What did she
imagine? That she was the only woman in his life? Just
because he looked at her with dove-grey eyes? Held her?
Make her feel seventeen again, desirable, like the only
woman in creation? Madness! It was rank adolescence to
fall for the illusion yet again. And had she really believed
all that stuff about his search for her when she had fled
Holcomb? He hadn't even stayed in for half an hour
tonight, before dashing out to enjoy himself. She must
be mad to fall for a line like that—of course he'd got the
letter she'd written him all those years ago, and was fully

aware of the contents. Youth was no excuse. What had he said himself? People don't change.

Well, it was true and he should know. Once a cad, always a cad.

Angrily she went through into the kitchen to make some cocoa. All the old habits of distrust, the feelings of having been let down, betrayed, were hard to break and needed little encouragement to reassert themselves. Coldly she resolved to ring his apartment on the private line every hour until he returned. She wouldn't find out where he'd been—unless he was so unashamed of his orgying that, uninvited, he told her himself—but she would find out *when* he returned. What satisfaction there would be in that she didn't care, just so long as she knew. Oh, Daniel, she wailed inwardly. Why? Again? Then she indulged in a bout of self-blame, telling herself that she had made it easy for him twice over, by falling so blindly for him. And she decided she couldn't ring, after all. It was silly—she knew that, anyway—and he was perfectly free, as a professional philanderer, to come and go as he pleased.

Just as she was about to trudge through into her bedroom with her mug of cocoa there was a buzz from the intercom. Somebody was ringing the front door. At this time of night? A quick glance at her watch told her it was nearly twenty to one. Even before she rushed to answer it, stumbling in her haste over one of the rugs, she knew it could only be one person.

'Yes?' she breathed into the mouthpiece.

'Claudia. I saw your light on. Is everything all right?'

'Yes. It was just a scare. He's as right as rain. I——'

'That's all I wanted to know.'

'Daniel!' She spoke loudly, as he seemed about to go away. 'Come up.'

'I don't think I'd better.'

'Why not? Do, please!' She pressed the buzzer to

release the door catch on the street door downstairs, and a few seconds later, to her profound relief, she heard him making his way up the stairs to the flat. Nervous now, when confession was imminent once again, she hesitated for only a moment before opening the inner door.

Then it swung back and Daniel came striding into the room.

A lock of straight blond hair hung in a dishevelled but heart-wrenchingly familiar way over his forehead as his gaze swept over the flat. He shot her a silvery glance that took in her bare feet and the fact that she was still fully dressed in the clothes she had been wearing earlier. There was no smile of any sort to soften the clean-cut, grimly etched lines of his face.

'I owe you an apology,' she began, thinking at the same time that more than mere apologies were due to him, if only the truth could be told, but before she could add to her opening, he cut in with an icy denial.

'You owe me nothing. I made a mistake, that's all.'

She felt her jaw drop. There was a harsh tone in his voice that was difficult to account for.

'W-what do you mean?' she managed to ask.

He replied with a harsh laugh. 'I forgot you were the type who turns on for everybody.'

She gazed speechlessly at him, not sure that she had heard correctly.

Struggling to make sense of it, she stuttered, 'That's not true. I-I don't understand——' Then, '*What* did you say?'

Enunciating with exaggerated clarity, he repeated, 'I forgot you were the type who turns on for everybody.'

Now fully awake to what he meant, she burst out heatedly, 'How dare you!' She moved a pace forward, with hands clenched.

'You sure as hell turn on for me, beautiful. But don't get me wrong. I'm not complaining. It's just that, as I might have said earlier, I prefer my pleasures exclusive——'

'How dare you say such a thing! You——'

'Yes?' His eyes sparked dangerously, daring her to spill out the ugliness he was taunting into existence.

With an effort, she merely pulled herself up and gave him a silent glare.

With an arrogance he did nothing to conceal, he strolled across the room towards her until he could reach out and drag her abruptly into his arms.

Resisting at first with some violence, she tried to pit her strength against his, but it was useless, he dwarfed her with his athlete's body. And besides that, there was the weakness she already knew when faced with the proximity of him.

'Come here, Claudia,' he murmured into her hair, pulling her body against his own with an unarguable gesture of assurance as she again made a show of resisting him. 'Come to me, lovely, yes . . .'

His touch, at first hard, as if to quell any resistance, became possessive, and his hands roamed her body quickly and intimately, whipping her senses to a frenzy of desire while at the same time drawing from her the need to resist this unexpected onslaught.

'No, Daniel!' She caught hold of both his hands in each of hers, as they gripped her possessively around her hips to draw her against him, so that she had no doubt how aroused he was, and tried to force them away, or at least push them to a less intimate part of her anatomy. But her puny strength was no match for him, and when she dug her long red nails sharply into the backs of his hands he merely laughed, the sound muffled in the hollow of her neck where his face was buried, and shifted them so that one hand held her hard up against his body, while the other began to slide hotly over her breasts, kneading them to a vibrating pitch of pleasure. She felt her senses respond at once, despite the strange silence in his manner that held something ominous. Regardless, her pelvis thrust against his, pulsing with the desire to know him once again and to be joined together in the ecstasy of love. His touch made her feel powerful enough to quell any extent of unreasonable anger he might feel—her touch would heal him.

Then she remembered Toby in the little bedroom just off the room they were in now, and she instinctively drew back.

'No, Daniel, please.'

'No means yes from you.' He bit the side of her neck and held her for a moment, teeth and lips making one molten whirlpool of radiant heat swamp her will. With an effort, she tried to drag herself back to reality, putting up both her hands to his shoulders to push him to one side. It was wasted effort, for he didn't seem to understand what she was trying to do, merely bringing his burning lips down over her half-open mouth and wreaking havoc on her will-power by the subtle teasing of his tongue inside her mouth. For a few minutes she was oblivious to everything but the vibrating of their two bodies, and it was only when he began to slip her panties down over her thighs that she managed to turn her head and whisper, 'No! Not now, darling, please . . . Toby's in the next room.'

Helpless to do anything to resist, she felt his warm hands continue to slide the flimsy lace down the length of her legs, and then his fingers were seeking out her most private realms, familiar, obdurately intent on arousing her to the heights of desire. She groaned with a fever of wanting their lovemaking to move to its climax, but still she tried to struggle against the suddenness of his advance. Somewhere at the back of her mind she felt something was wrong—the familiar endearing warmth he emanated was gone, and instead he seemed scarcely aware of who she was, as if motivated by blind emotion. It made her raise her face from where she had buried it

in the sleek muscles of his shoulder to mutter hoarsely,
'Toby. He's——'

'Damn Toby!' Daniel replied roughly without looking up. 'Do you want me?'

She opened her eyes fully, and gazed up into his face.
'Oh, Daniel yes, I want you, but——'

'Even with Toby in the next room?' he muttered, not
letting her finish her sentence. His hands had stopped
their pulsing exploration and were sliding silkily over
her heated skin, massaging her with undulating movements to match his own rhythmic swaying, as he
watched for her response.

'I'd rather he wasn't quite . . . so close,' she muttered,
half turning her head to avoid the gaze he had at last
fixed on her. There was something disconcerting in it, as
if now he had managed to pull his glance towards her
there was a barrier of some sort standing between them.
It was cold. Unfriendly to the point of hostility.

Then he spoke, though it was more like a small snarl.
'I bet you would,' he said softly, 'though if you try to
keep your moans of pleasure quiet I'm sure you would
get away with it.' He gave a harsh laugh. 'I suppose for
someone like you it adds a bit of spice to the occasion.
Did you ask them to give him knock-out pills at the
hospital?'

'This is crazy!' Claudia gaped at him, stunned by the
savagery of his attack, her mouth, which had been
slightly open in helpless pleasure, now dropping in frank
astonishment, and her flesh, over-heated, seeming to
cool rapidly as icy fingers stalked it.

'See how easy it is?' Daniel ground out. 'I guessed,
when you switched off so rapidly this evening on hearing
about loverboy, that you would switch back on just as
quickly.'

This time, when his hands swept tantalisingly along
the lines of her half-naked body, there was no hot touch
of desire in them, merely the cynical contact with

something to be briefly possessed. It chilled Claudia to the soul. His words made no sense. Then, through the haze of her befuddled thoughts, she remembered what she had resolved to tell him earlier, which only the failure to make contact with him and the shock of his appearance now had prevented.

'Daniel, let me explain——' she began.

His laugh was chilling to hear. 'It's too late for explanations. You should have explained your disappearing act thirteen years ago. I was a boy then, capable of being hurt. This time I don't wound so easily, Claudia. I know the magic your wide blue eyes can weave, but you've lost your power to bind me. I can see you for what you really are——'

Suddenly ashamed, she saw herself as she must look through his eyes—dark hair falling in disarray from its clip, mascara-smudged eyes, blouse gaping open to reveal her breasts, skirt rucked up to her waist, and, most humiliating, lace panties trampled underfoot. While he, despite his apparent aim to get her into bed, remained fully clothed, not immaculately, but in less disarray than she was and with all his clothes in their proper place.

A blush of humiliation sped like flame over her skin, and her eyes glistened with a mixture of shame and anger with herself.

'How could I have let you fool me—again!' she cried, shakily grabbing for the hem of her skirt to try to drag it back into place.

'No, don't be a spoilsport,' he mocked, gripping her hands to stop them in their tidying up. 'You look beautifully debauched like that—I simply wish dear Toby wasn't liable to come bursting in to break things up at the crucial moment. Or is he used to your carryings-on?'

'Dan, it's not like that!'

'Save me your blatant lies, Claudia. I've seen you for

what you are, thank God, before it's too late.'

Before she knew what he was doing, his two hands released hers, slid once possessively over her heated body, to taunt the flesh beneath the gaping clothes, then his lips came down crushingly over hers, stopping the breath in her body and forcing her lips against her teeth. His tongue probed once, strong and deep into her mouth, then with a similar suddenness he relinquished his hold so that she almost fell to her knees.

By the time she had recovered he was already at the door.

'Don't bother to see me out,' he mocked. 'I'm sure you'll want to get back to your invalid lover.'

With a horrible cry of anguish, Claudia flung herself towards the door, but it clicked in her face and she threw herself, sobbing, against it. She could hear him descending the stairs two at a time. By the time she had pulled herself together sufficiently to go after him it was too late. His name echoed down the empty stairwell. Then there came a slam as the street door banged shut behind him.

He was drunk, Claudia guessed, though this would have been really no excuse even if it had been true, and there had been only the slight whiff of Scotch on his breath, equal to one after-dinner drink. Even so, a fear took hold of her that he was too drunk to drive, that he would crash his car before she could get to him to tell him the truth. Suddenly anger riled through her at the insulting lie he had uttered about her. And then she excused him, because she could see how he had arrived at such a monstrous perversion of the truth. In a torrent of emotion, she resolved to drive out after him, accost him at the hotel, force him to listen to her while she told him her side.

Then she remembered Toby, how she dared not leave him, just in case the hospital had made a mistake to let him out so soon, just in case he had failed to tell her everything about his accident that day. There was only one thing for it, and that was to buckle down her patience, to wait until he got back to the hotel, and then to speak some sense into him over the phone.

So telling herself, she undressed properly, washed and cleaned her teeth, then, hugging the phone to her, climbed beneath the duvet and dialled the now familiar number. As earlier, it went unanswered. She tried the night porter again. And again the same response.

'Mr Sinnington has not yet returned to the hotel.'

She asked for a message to be left. 'Urgent. Please contact Claudia Gray.'

Long hours of the night passed, and nothing happened. She tried his private line again, but there was still no response. She gave up for the night and fell into a troubled sleep.

At eight, having lain awake long before that, she rang reception again. It was a woman's voice. The receptionist with the mahogany hair, she guessed.

'Your message has been passed on to Mr Sinnington,' she was told.

She waited until nine-thirty, then, nerves at snapping-point, made her way down to the salon.

'You look pale,' Susie greeted her with cheerful honesty.

'I feel pale. Toby's upstairs, sleeping like the proverbial log.'

To Susie's raised eyebrows, she explained, 'Apparently he was in some sort of scrape at school, and was whisked off to hospital in an ambulance with his best friend—much to their delight, it seems.' She plastered a smile on to her face. 'He looks as fit as a cartload of monkeys to me, but they must have had their reasons for such drastic action. Perhaps they were afraid he would eat all the jam sandwiches. Anyway, I may have to dash out mid-morning to pop him back into school, if that's going to fit in with you——'

'I don't see why you don't keep him off the rest of the day, and spend the time at Lake House,' suggested Susie, her concern at Claudia's appearance showing. 'I can manage here, and you were talking about some paperwork you wanted to finish. May as well do it there, in comfort . . . You look tired, Claudia. Are you worried about him?'

'No,' she replied honestly. 'He seems all right. But I didn't sleep much last night.'

'Go home for the day, then. You have no reason not to.'

Claudia had scarcely been able to think straight enough to prepare even a simple breakfast for herself, and she wearily passed a hand over her hair. 'Perhaps I'll ring the school and see if there's any urgent reasons why he should be there, rather than with me.'

Exams were over. It was the last winding-down week of term, anyway, and Toby had certainly been sleeping soundly when she'd looked in on him. His escapade had probably taken more out of him than she realised.

She got through to the school secretary, Mrs Moxon. Her manner was most effusive. 'And is our young hero feeling all right this morning?' she almost drooled.

Claudia was taken aback. Toby was well liked, but this was extreme, wasn't it? 'Toby?' she repeated, just in case they thought she was some other mum. 'Yes, he's still asleep. I wondered if he might have the day off——'

'The Head suggested it might be best to do that. Until all the excitement dies down.'

'Oh?' Claudia felt out of her depth. Last night had been more of a strain than she had realised, and it was stopping her from hearing the sense in things. The secretary added to her confusion when she told her. 'The Press rang, but I told them he was unavailable for comment. I believe that's the correct phrase. No doubt they'll be getting in touch with you. Apparently they want photographs. And why not? It's excellent for the school. Tell him we're all thinking of him.' And with that she rang off.

'Press? Photographs?' She wrinkled her brow at Susie. 'What's been going on? Have I been on another planet for the last few days?'

'You can say that again,' Susie laughed. 'Ever since you-know-who came on the scene——'

'Susie, shut up.' She turned to go. 'By the way,' she poked her head back round the door, 'if we-all-know-who——' She faltered, unable to bring herself to say his name aloud. 'If he happens to ring—would you mind rerouting the call to Lake House? In fact——' She stopped altogether, an idea forcing its way through the jumble of emotions. 'If he does happen to call, ask him to come over there, would you? As soon as possible. Got that?'

Susie gave a cheshire-cat grin. 'I've got it all right, sweetie. And I must say, it's high time we saw some action in that area. Lake House it is.'

Action? Claudia raised her eyebrows at that, then without even attempting to explain she wended her way back upstairs. She found Toby sitting up in bed, looking around blearily, as if not quite sure how he had managed to surface in his bed here at the flat.

Pushing thoughts of Daniel to one side with an immense effort, she called to Toby from the doorway, 'Well, me lad, how would you like the day off school? What's left of it, that is——'

When she had disentangled herself from his arms and legs, she considered how easy it was to make him happy.

'Now,' she said, sternly, settling back on to the bed, 'What's been going on behind my back? Why are the Press ringing the school about you? What *have* you been up to?'

Little by little, with a charming blush making him look at least three years younger, Toby confessed.

'It was all an accident, really,' he began. 'Pugsie started to rescue a calf, as I told you. Then the silly idiot lost his footing on one of the rocks. I told him not to stand on the green, weedy bits. Well, he just went under. And then he got swept down a sluice and into the Falls. It's white water. I could see he'd cracked his head on one of the rocks and didn't know what he was doing. I could hardly just stand by and watch him drown, so I ran like crazy along the bank to where I knew he'd be coming down and then I went in——' He gave her a sidelong glance. 'I only went up to my waist, honest, Mum.'

'All right, love. You're safe. The pair of you. That's all that matters now. What happened next?' she asked, suspicions not fully laid to rest.

'We were in luck. I managed to hang on to him and we both slid down a bit, and then I got a bit of a grip on some overhanging branches. And then we managed to get close into the bank so they could pull us up. It was nothing. What do they want a photo for? I won't get into trouble, will I?'

'They're not police mugshots, you clot!' She cuddled him, moved by the mixture of grown-up pride and little-boy defensiveness that was at odds with his gangly grown-up look.

They left the salon for Lake House before lunch, but before they could even reach the car, a dark green limousine drew up beside them and asked, 'Toby Hampshire?' A Press card flashed. And then and there a photographer climbed from the car and asked Toby, and, with a sudden inspirational glance, Claudia, to pose for a quick picture. It was all over in a few seconds, much to Toby's disappointment, and they were at Lake House no more than twenty minutes later.

Daniel had not returned her call. Just to make sure, she phoned Susie.

'Not a peep, love. I'll let you know straight away if he gets in touch.'

With a heart like lead, Claudia stood at the french windows and looked out across the gardens. If Daniel could be as hostile as this over the mistaken assumption that she had a lover, what would his reaction be like if he knew what she was really trying to cover up?

Toby's blond head was moving above the top of the neatly clipped laurel hedge that marked the edge of the path round the side of the house. She watched it for a second or too, thinking how rapidly he was growing when she gave a start, for Toby had been in the kitchen when she'd last seen him, rummaging like a starving man through the fridge, afternoon tea being over nearly half an hour ago. How then could he——'

'Toby?' she called.

'I'm not touching the pork pie.' The answer came back smartly from the direction of the kitchen.

She sped out of the sitting-room, and Toby jerked up guiltily as she appeared in the doorway.

'Honestly, I'm not!' he told her reproachfully. 'I've only eaten a bit of the crust that fell off.'

'Oh, Toby, darling. Eat it all if you want. Do!'

He looked at her as if she were mad. 'Do you really mean it?'

Without answering, she swept him into her arms, fear surging through her, making her turn guiltily just as Toby had done a moment earlier. Someone crunched over the gravel outside and came to a stop at the open kitchen door, catching them like that, arms round each other, the blond head of the boy a good four inches above the dark one of his mother.

Toby, pork pie in hand, glanced rapidly from Claudia to the blond stranger gazing in hostile fashion at the pair of them, and was for once silent.

Claudia and Daniel exchanged glances. He held a newspaper in his hand, holding it out like a kind of talisman, but he didn't speak.

'Daniel, look——' It was Claudia who was the first to break the silence. She took a deep gulping breath, stepped forward, but still kept a tight hold on Toby, as if she expected him to try to escape before she'd finished speaking. 'I want you to meet Toby—my son.'

Toby had the good manners to deposit the pork pie on the table and wipe his hands on a cloth before holding one of them out to clasp one of Daniel's

'Toby, this is Daniel Sinnington.' There was a slight pause, into which Claudia could mentally hear the words she might have added as loudly as if they had been spoken through a foghorn. Then, with a sudden relaxation of the coldness that had characterised him so far, Daniel stepped forward and took the boy's hand warmly in his own.

CHAPTER NINE

'WELL done, Toby.' Daniel indicated the paper he was holding. 'I've just seen the photograph of you and your mother in the early edition.' He shot a black look at Claudia on the word 'mother', which she did her best to ignore.

'Thank you, sir.' Toby looked abashed, then gave Daniel a reciprocal scrutiny. 'I've seen you before,' he announced. 'You called in at my barbecue last Saturday.'

'It was yours, was it?' Daniel gave Claudia another piercing glance that clearly told her there was going to be a lot of explaining ahead. He turned back to Toby, asking keenly. 'Was it your birthday?'

'Toby, I thought you were busy?' cut in Claudia nervously.

'I am? Oh, yes! Sorry, Mum!' Grinning impishly, Toby withdrew with an example of tact far beyond his years. But before he disappeared entirely he remembered the pork pie. Retrieving it from the table he called cheerfully, 'See you later, sir!' and to Claudia's immense relief he strolled off in the direction of his den at the bottom of the garden without more ado.

'Neat,' observed Daniel, leaning against the doorpost and treating Claudia to a black stare. 'Does he always do as he's told?'

'It depends on whether he's trying to make a good impression or not,' she answered with a nervous smile. She felt like a small, very defenceless animal, waiting for

149

the big cat to pounce.

'He's a big lad,' Daniel continued with feline stealth. 'I can't quite believe he's your son. But,' he added thoughtfully, 'the eyes are unmistakable. You must have married almost straight after our little "*affaire*".' He accented the word like a Frenchman, and somehow managed to give it a sleazy link with their embarrassing encounter on the previous night.

Claudia turned away. The warmth with which he had exchanged words with Toby had gone now and was replaced by an air of unmistakable malevolence. In this present mood, the slightest remark would send him flying through the roof. It did not create the calm, civilised ambience which was required to tell him what she had decided to tell him.

'Why have you come here?' she demanded tightly, keeping her back to him, while she pretended to tidy the kitchen.

Without answering her question he replied, 'I feel like a vacuum cleaner salesman standing out here. May I come inside?'

She thrust a quick glance over her shoulder. 'I'm sorry. Of course.' It was mere politeness. She wanted nothing more than that he should leave. She braced herself and asked, 'Would you like a drink?'

'What are you offering?'

'What would you like?' Claudia raised her glance to his.

'Do you need to ask?' His eyes locked with hers.

'Am I supposed to be a mind reader?'

'Can't you read minds?'

'Why should I bother?'

'Why not?'

'We could go on like this for ever,' she exploded, still unable to drop her glance.

'Would you like to?' His voice seemed to deepen.

'Don't, Daniel. What do you want?'

'An explanation.'

'I meant, to drink.'

'I'll take the drink, only if I can have an explanation afterwards.'

'I don't know what you mean——'

'Shall I say it in Swahili?'

'Don't, Daniel——'

'Don't what? Show off my Swahili?'

She couldn't help smiling. 'I don't know whether you're still raging like you were last night.'

'Only inwardly.' He moved like liquid across the kitchen towards her.

Her senses bristled and she said quickly, 'I-I'll get you something. Tea? Coffee? Or something——?'

When he put both his hands on the worktop on either side of her, her words trailed away, and he effectively pinned her to the spot by his action without so much as touching her.

'... something stronger?' he murmured, finishing her question for her. His expression was unreadable. She nodded, words beyond her reach. His nearness brought nothing but confusion.

'What about Scotch and soda?' he suggested blandly. As if satisfied with the effect his nearness had on her, or reluctant to betray the fact that despite his recent harsh judgement she could still in her turn affect him, he slid his hands away and stepped back. She slithered out of reach at once.

'It's—it's in the sitting-room,' she faltered.

'Yes, I remember,' he remarked as he shadowed her across the hall. 'Or was that in your friends' house? They're so similar, it'd be easy to get them mixed up.'

Claudia felt a rosy tinge paint her cheeks. 'I didn't lie to you,' she countered, to cover the shame she felt at being caught out in her ealier subterfuge, even though the 'lie' had merely amounted to letting him jump to conclusions. 'It's not my fault you're prone to make these wild assumptions.'

'True,' he agreed unexpectedly, 'but you're certainly to blame for engineering situations to create a certain—shall we say—impression . . .'

'If you cast your mind back,' she replied cuttingly, in tones that suggested she doubted whether in fact he had a mind, 'you gatecrashed a party I was giving for my son. So you can hardly say I engineered it.'

'But you failed to correct me when I made such a blundering assessment, didn't you?' His grey eyes lashed silkily over her face, as if he had actually reached out to taunt her with his physical presence. Pointedly she forced her glance away and pretended to search in the cabinet for two glasses.

'To your left,' he remarked helpfully, watching her efforts.

'I know.'

'You always seem confused when you see me,' he went on.

'Do you wonder?' she broke out bitterly, slopping Scotch into two glasses, then standing, bemused, at a loss to remember what she had been going to add next.

'Soda, perhaps?' he suggested evenly, again observing her predicament. Then before she could say anything he added, 'On the shelf to your right.'

'Stop it! I know what I'm doing.'

'Don't you always? The cool, collected Claudia Gray. The lady in control.'

'Does that worry you?' she gritted, squirting soda

into her glass so hard that she lost half the Scotch. Before she could take a pace towards the kitchen to get a cloth, he leaned forward, with a sky-blue handkerchief produced like magic, and deftly wiped up the puddle of whisky from the cabinet top.

'And now you've made a thorough hash of that,' he remarked, 'come and sit down and answer a few questions. And no, it wouldn't worry me if it were the whole truth. I like women who know what they're about. I've never liked cabbages.'

Silently she handed him the squat glass, wishing for nothing more than the courage to throw it over him. Resisting the impulse with an effort, she moved instead to one of the big armchairs beside the open windows, and plumped down with knees locked tightly together and lips set in an unforgiving line.

'If you imagine I'm going to sit here and be cross-questioned by you, Daniel,' she began, 'you've another think coming. Anybody would think you were working for the police.'

'Hardly that,' he replied taking a seat directly opposite her on the sofa, 'but, as managing director of Country House Hotels, I feel I ought to have a few rather disquieting questions cleared up. After all, we're sinking quite a lot of capital into the salon franchise, don't you agree? We need to know our money's safe.'

'Oh, nice one!' she exclaimed ironically. 'So you think the financial hook gives you *carte blanche* to pry into my sex life.'

'Do you have one?'

'God, you're insulting! Get out!' She tried to rise to her feet, with the intention of showing him the door, but anticipating her intention he rose more rapidly than she did and gently held her back in the chair with one hand.

'Don't spill your drink,' he mocked, as she twisted her head left and right in an attempt to find a place to set her glass down so that she could push him out of the way. He was so close, crouching over her, that their faces were almost touching. 'Listen, Claudia, I didn't come here to pry or to insult you. Understand?'

'Why are you here, then?' she managed to croak, furious to feel herself so helpless.

'I'm here in answer to your invitation,' he answered simply.

Having had her brisk request to Susie pushed to the back of her mind with his sudden materialisation on her doorstep just now, without the promised warning telephone call, she could only mutter glumly, 'I'm surprised you took any notice.'

His next words made her think again. 'There was a record number of phone calls recorded by reception last night, and a verbal message when I went down just after eight . . . I assume all the calls must have been from you and, judging by their number and frequency, it suggested a matter of some urgency. I could hardly ignore it——'

'If you'd been in your suite at a normal time,' she cut in, 'I wouldn't have had to waste so many calls.' She felt stupid. Why hadn't she realised that all messages were recorded? What did he imagine she had been up to?

'I could only assume you were off your head with drink last night,' she informed him stiffly to cover herself. 'I simply rang to see if you got back all right.'

'I went for a drive and when I came back I put the phone on silent as usual. So yes, I got back all right. Did you care?'

'Not a damn,' she remarked, avoiding the piercing brightness of his eyes.

'Strange behaviour for someone who doesn't care a damn.'

'Yes,' she agreed shortly, refusing to admit even to herself that his words were enough cause to revise her previous opinion of him in one clean sweep—no all-night rave-up, just safe in his room where he should have been.

His voice dropped to a murmur and he said, 'When you do learn to show your concern consistently, it's going to be wonderful for some lucky fellow——'

'And it won't be you!' she capped.

He gave a faint smile. 'I admit I was in two minds whether to bother contacting you—it was only when the photograph caught my eye that I realised the situation needed looking into.'

'I can't see why,' she retorted, foolishly. Sure enough, he took it as an invitation to tell her. Spelling it out as if to an infant, he perched on the edge of her chair and said, 'Well, it's like this—you were pretending to keep me at arm's length last night because of Toby. And, as seems to be your habit, you deliberately allowed me to believe he was your lover, not your son.'

'That was you—jumping to conclusions again.'

'Oh, so it's all my fault, is it?'

'It was you who misunderstood,' she went on. 'I wanted to tell you, but you didn't give me a chance. And,' she added, 'that's why I invited you up in the first place——'

'But you didn't breathe a word!'

'How could I?' she raised her voice. 'You were still in a rage because I'd dashed of to the hospital——'

'Out of my arms,' he glinted, 'and into those of your stricken lover!'

'As you *thought*!' she corrected, then quickly conceded, 'At the hospital I realised I owed you an explanation. I was just too distraught to think straight after the call came . . .' Her huge eyes were unveiled for a moment as she looked up at him, but then the dark lashes swept down again, hiding their expression. 'There was still no need to behave in that—that beastly fashion,' she muttered.

'I admit, I lost control. You make me do that. It's not an excuse. I'm sorry.'

He bent to kiss the top of her head and explained, 'All the time you were at that damned hospital I was imagining sick-bed reconciliation scenes—it was obvious that this lover I thought you had was less than central to events. But I imagined that in true female fashion you'd take one look at him lying at death's door and go all gooey over him. So when I finally saw you I just flipped. It took all my self-control not to go barging in like a madman to the room he was sleeping in to confront him.'

'Toby would have been surprised, to put it mildy.'

'Yes, Toby.' Daniel looked thoughtful and Claudia shivered at the sudden significance his name had acquired. 'Now, *why* didn't you tell me about him?' he asked.

'When he saw you at the barbecue,' she went on chattily before he could stop her, 'he got the very mistaken impression that you were OK.' Then she broke off, hastily covering tracks that were again surely leading on to ·dangerous ground by adding lamely, 'which just goes to show how impressions can mislead.'

Daniel gave her a pointed look. 'How old *is* he?'

'What the hell's it got to do with you? Leave Toby out of this!' she whipped back, prickles of apprehension brushing her spine.

'OK. OK. I guess you hate to admit you got yourself involved with someone else so soon after us.' He paused. 'Or perhaps not even "after" us at all . . .' He swung up from the arm of the chair, face grim, voice, when he spoke again, offhand. 'Idiotic to get married so young, wasn't it? No wonder it didn't last!'

To this, Claudia made no reply.

'Still, the coast is clear now,' he stated, dropping the words into her silence like silver coins.

'C-clear?' she stammered, her heart swooping wildly.

'It must have been difficult—a single parent, career woman, a place like this to keep up. Even though your old man perhaps left you comfortably off?' Her pursed lips made him offer a mocking apology. 'No sorry, I suppose that comes into the category of prying again, doesn't it?'

'Yes,' she clipped. His words had once more led her into the trap of appearing to engineer situations so that he fell for the wrong conclusion. Reluctant to edge any closer to the truth, she couldn't resist satisfying her curiosity, so she asked him with an enigmatic little smile, 'What am I, then, Daniel—widow or divorcée?'

'Do I get a prize if I get it right?'

'No.'

'I'm not playing, then.'

Just at that moment, Toby skidded up to the french windows and hovered ostentatiously outside until Claudia was forced to look up. 'What is it, darling?' she asked, relieved to be let off the hook of Daniel's suspicions for a moment.

'There's a fantastic breeze. D'you think I could take the boat out by myself?'

Reluctant to have to help him drag the sailing dinghy

from the boathouse while wearing a pale silk dress, she told him, 'I'll have to get changed first. Can it wait a few minutes?' She meant until Daniel left, as there seemed nothing more to be said between them. Certainly she had no intention of laying herself open to further speculations about her past. And now he knew she had a son, she hoped he would imagine there was nothing more to be said.

To her surprise, Daniel raised his blond head with an expression of interest.

'Want a hand, fella?' he asked, his manner suddenly mellowing.

'Oh, you'll get dirty.' Claudia glanced at his spotless white denims and pale grey cotton jacket. 'It's in a rather spidery boathouse at the bottom of the garden——' But Toby spoilt it all by giving an India whoop as soon as Daniel offered.

'I've survived this far. I'm sure I can see off a few spiders,' he remarked ironically, rising straight to his feet and depositing his used glass tidily on a table as he followed Toby out.

Surprised by the speed with which he had offered his help, she strolled to the windows to watch the two blond heads disappear between the trees. A residual suspicion formed in her mind that Daniel only wanted to fish for answers to his questions. But after a moment's thought, she decided to leave him to it—what Toby could tell him was zilch.

Instead she went up to her dressing-room. She would change into something more casual. No doubt she would have to help Toby bring the boat up later. Knowing him of old he would be out on the lake until the wind dropped around tea time, when Daniel would have long since departed.

Aware that she felt irrationally pleased to have discovered that Daniel hadn't been out all last night, living it up with countless girlfriends—for she believed what he had told her without reservation—she had a half-smile on her face as she rifled through her wardrobe. Her eye alighted on a pair of snug blue jeans and, cautioned by the look in Daniel's eyes when he'd seen her in a skimpy T-shirt, she donned a baggy red and white striped shirt, wearing it loose outside her jeans in order to conceal her voluptuous figure even more. A comfortable pair of chunky white trainers completed her outfit.

Expecting to find Daniel hovering by the door, ready to leave, she went down to the kitchen, surprised to find no one there. As she crossed to the back door she picked up the newspaper Daniel had dropped on to the table and flicked over to have a look at the picture of Toby and herself. Mother and son. A Press photographer's hurried snap.

The caption brought a gasp to her lips, though, for there was more.

'Schoolboy hero in Falls rescue drama,' shrieked the headlines. Rapidly scanning the rest of it, she finished up with a proud smile all over her face. How like Toby to play down his starring role in a drama like that! Unless the article was sheer fantasy, he had rescued not only Julian but two other lads as well—swimming out into the Falls with a rope around his waist no less than three times to bring them safely to the bank. Fear at what might have been the outcome was stifled by regret for the harsh words she had dealt him over the incident earlier in the day. It made her head straight out to the garden.

As she came within earshot of the boathouse she could

hear two voices talking nineteen to the dozen, and, rounding a clump of rhododendrons she saw them heads down, rigging the boat like old friends. The sight brought a pang to her heart. Not for the first time, she wondered if Toby truly regretted never having had a man around to play father to him. Did he miss having a good, tough, no-nonsense male figure to talk to? She couldn't be everything to him—but she often felt the strain of continually trying for the impossible.

Waving the paper above her head, she approached across the turf. Daniel spun his head suddenly and she caught his glistening, emotion-charged look. He obviously found her appearance unexpected. Trying to ignore him she held up the paper. 'You're a dark horse, Tobes. Is this all true? Why didn't you tell me?'

'I guessed you'd be mad at me,' he replied simply.

'There are different kinds of "mad at"!' she exclaimed. 'And one comes from sheer fear at losing someone you love——' She stopped abruptly. As the words fell from her lips, her eyes had swivelled involuntarily to meet Daniel's. There was no need for words. She knew at once that she had hit on the cause of his animal rage the previous night. He thought he had lost her to another man. She hadn't believed him when he had hinted at it a few moments ago, but now the expression startled on to his face swept away her doubts.

Suddenly the urgency of her desire to set the record straight increased, but she still shuddered at the implications. Her own fear—the old one of losing him completely in a rerun of her earlier loss—swept icily up her body with a dead hand.

'Claudia, are you all right?' Daniel was beside her in a trice. 'Steady,' he murmured in her ear, resting an arm around her waist. 'You're suffering shock at reading about the danger he was in—but papers always exaggerate. You know that . . .'

She gave him a wan smile. She could explain later, if necessary. 'I'm all right,' she lied. The enormity of what she was going to do sent her scurrying metaphorically for cover. She brushed aside his concern with a quick shake of her head.

'She's already for launching, Dan. Are you coming?' Toby interrupted.

'Helm or crew?' demanded Daniel tersely, prising himself away from Claudia's side with a last unconcealed look of concern.

'You don't have to, Daniel!' called Claudia to his retreating back. A silvery smile over the shoulder was his only response.

Mystified as to why he was being so affable all of a sudden, she watched them splash the boat down from the bank into the water, then saw them skim away across the lake as the breeze caught the sail. With Toby at the helm, the dinghy was rock-steady and she watched long enough to see it go about and run downwind until they were just two black dots against the diminishing red sail.

As she made her way back towards the house, It crossed her mind that by the time they came back in it would be nearly supper time. Dared she risk extending an invitation to Daniel, and prolonging the time they spent in each other's company? Even now, to borrow a metaphor from the yachting world, she was sailing close to the wind. The trouble was, she dared not trust herself with him, for obvious reasons—and nor dared she trust him. But talk to him openly she must.

They were out for nearly two hours in all, and it was only when the sun began to set, bringing with it a drop in the wind, that she saw the red sail begin to head back towards the shore.

Standing on the terrace with an aroma of home-cooked food drifting through the kitchen door, she watched them land, and then listened to their distant laughter with a smile of something like contentment on her face. I want things to remain like this for ever, she thought—sunlight speckling the garden, happy voices somewhere beyond the trees, the two people I love most in all the world coming home to me.

She shook herself. She was becoming soft. Her disillusionment would be all the greater if she didn't control her gooey sentiments right now.

'Are we eating outside?' demanded Toby as he came bounding up the garden beside Daniel.

'Would you like to?' she half turned to Daniel, afraid to ask him outright in case he said no—and perversely afraid to ask in case he said yes, as well. She searched his face for any sign of change in it, but he seemed the same as ever.

'Sounds good,' he replied easily, apparently unaware of the conflict raging inside her. 'Do you want a hand?'

'Just make sure Toby shows you where you can freshen up and——'

'Make sure he does the same?' he finished for her. They shared adult smiles over the top of Toby's head. It caused Claudia an involuntary pang. When had she ever been able to share the travails of bringing up an energetic boy with anyone? It was a lack that continually gnawed at her.

When they both came back down, Claudia had already put the finishing touches to the table on the terrace. She lit the lamp they always used for al fresco suppers and went back into the kitchen to fetch the casserole. Daniel followed her in.

'I would have brought a bottle of wine if I'd know things were going to turn out like this, Claudia. Have I time to go and——?'

'I've already done it. I hope you approve.'

Daniel followed her glance. 'You've even decorked it——' he read the label '—and show excellent taste, too. Is there nothing I can do for you?' His eyes conveyed a greater depth than the lightness of his tone suggested, but she brushed aside the deeper meaning with all its implications, and replied as lightly as she could, 'You can organise that batch of bread, if you like!'

He gave a mock grimace. 'Was that all I meant?'

Before she could think of a reply, he picked up the basket, remarking, 'You're expecting to feed an army?'

'You haven't seen Toby at work,' she replied, pleased to be on more neutral ground.

'He's delightful. May I borrow him some time?'

'Borrow?' She looked startled.

'Don't worry—I don't mean to make him work in my salt mines. It's just that I sail a fast little craft off the coast, and he'd be a very handy crew.'

'Ask him—he'd love it!' she exclaimed, then bit her lip. Step by step, it seemed their paths were becoming entwined despite her intentions. 'He's actually rather busy at school these days . . .'

'I was thinking about the summer holidays,' he countered. 'Accompanied by his mother.'

'Well . . . maybe,' she replied feebly. But wait, she added silently, until you've heard the truth.

'He was telling me about the wind-sailing course he's going on soon. You seem to do very well by him, Claudia,' he went on conversationally.

'Hm!' Claudia dismissed the compliment with a wave of her hand. It was no good trying to explain her feelings of guilt that she was never doing enough for him, but she made a half-hearted attempt. 'I sometimes wonder if he regrets not having a father,' she admitted. 'I try to compensate, but it's not always easy to know if one's doing the right thing.'

'It's hardly your fault his old man isn't around,' Daniel replied carefully, suddenly fixing his piercing grey eyes on her.

Isn't it? she wanted to shout. Isn't it my fault? But with an effort she bit back the words and lifted her face in a tremulous smile. As he looked as if he was going to say more, she launched quickly into a description of the adventure holiday lined up for Toby next month, and in the middle of it Toby himself came clattering down, homing in on the oven-hot bread like a starveling, and the danger was temporarily avoided.

'Slap his paws if he gets them near this food before he's sitting properly at table,' ordered Claudia shakily, reaching for the oven glove so she could take the casserole from out of the oven and achieve some semblance of normality over her bucking emotions.

'You heard, fella, scarper!' grinned Daniel, and miraculously Toby did as he was told. As soon as they were alone again, he observed, 'It puzzles me why you tried to keep quiet about him all this time. If he were my son, I'd want the whole world to know ...'

'Let's eat before it gets cold,' she muttered, hurriedly grabbing for the serving dish and beating a hasty retreat outside.

It was a simple home-made herb soup with sorrel and lovage freshly picked from the garden, followed by hot French bread, parsley butter and a rich *cassoulet*, rounded off by ice-cream for Toby and cheese and biscuits with freshly roasted French coffee for Daniel and herself.

Afterwards, they all sat contentedly replete in the crimson glow of a spectacular sunset that lingered as if it would never end. The carefully inconsequential conversation that had taken place throughout the meal gave way to a contented silence as they watched the unfolding kaleidoscope of colours transform the sky from gold through all the gradations of red to palest amethyst. The last colours lingered so long that Toby was moved to exclaim, 'The earth's stopped moving!' at which Daniel exchanged a meaningful and very adult glance with Claudia that made her blush.

'We'll have to see what we can do about that, won't we?' he murmured wickedly.

She was thankful when Toby's head began to droop and, the sunset show almost over, she could send him of to bed. Hoping that Daniel would be as easily despatched to his own bed, she came back down after warning Toby to clean his teeth.

She began to set about clearing the table, annoyed when he didn't leap up to take his leave at once. If he didn't leave straight away, she would have to stop this cowardly evasion and speak out.

'I'll have to go and kiss him goodnight in a moment,' she announced pointedly, so that the message was loud and clear. But when he stood up beside her it was obvious that he was not to be so easily managed, and in fact had got quite a different message from her words.

'I hope the goodnight kisses extend to me,' he said softly.

'Emphatically not.' Claudia stepped back from where

her tidying up had led her dangerously close to where he stood.

'Shame.' Daniel pulled a face. Then on a different note he murmured, 'It's been a beautiful evening, in every way.' He made no attempt to follow up on his earlier words, but instead looked out with a thoughtful frown across the lawns to where the lake lay like a pool of molten gold behind the spidery silhouette of the trees.

'Shall we do this again?' he asked.

Claudia took a step along the terrace until she reached the edge of the grass. Night was closing in around them now, veiling the garden in purple and indigo, revealing mysteries unapparent in the bright light of day. She would have to speak out. But once again she let cowardice take over.

'It's no good, Daniel.' She half turned to where he was still standing beside the white garden table. 'I-I simply haven't time for deep involvements. And besides, I don't want Toby to become too attached to you—he could only be hurt when the affair was over and you said goodbye.'

'*He* would be hurt?' His mouth twisted momentarily. 'And what about you?'

I would be devastated, she thought, but the words stuck in her throat.

'Well?' he persisted.

'I-I would feel upset, naturally, if——' She shrugged, unable to go on.

'If I deserted you again.'

Her head jerked up. Thanking the darkness for concealing the sudden start of emotion to her face, she managed to stammer, 'W-what makes you say that? You believe *I* left you . . .'

'But you say you wrote to me—and that I never replied.'

'Yes—I think—I thought that was what had happened.'

'And you fear I'll leave you again—even though you now realise I didn't chuck you then at all. On the contrary . . .

His voice flowed like liquid honey, but she stabbed out, 'Don't, Dan. Please don't rake up the past. It's over.'

'But is it?' Still he didn't move towards her. Instead, she felt the force of his will focused unwaveringly on her.

'What was in that letter you wrote to me, Claudia?'

When she didn't reply, despite eyes that were drawn hypnotically to his like a snake charmed by a flute player, he murmured, 'Come here.' The words were thrown like a silken rope between them and, as surely as if he had been hauling on the other end, she felt her limbs begin to carry her slowly across the intervening grass towards him. Only when she was within a yard of him could she force herself to come to a standstill. Reluctantly she allowed her glance to hold his for a moment longer, fighting the power that could destroy her will.

'Come to me, Claudia,' he repeated softly, lifting one hand to her. As if the air was alive with pulsing volts of electricity, she moved a little closer, still reluctant, cautious, frightened to take the last irrevocable step.

'Come to me, Claudia,' he repeated huskily, then, his silver glance dissolving her fears, she knew they were as nothing against the raging desire to throw her trembling body into the flames of love. She felt she would stop living altogether if she was prevented from joining with him, for living within his ambience was all she would ever need. Words, explanations, all that could wait.

The last trace of resistance quelled with such frightening speed, she resolved to settle for whatever the present held, sliding with a sense of inevitability into the sheltering warmth of his embrace. A small sound of satisfaction escaped him as Daniel's arms locked around her, pressing her head against his shoulder while he rocked her back and forth in his arms.

What had started as a feeling of completeness at the instant of physical contact, soon created its own need with the satisfying of that first desire, so that the kisses he moulded to her face seemed too little to express the vibrant urgency of a greater hunger.

With a dreamlike accord of wills, they moved away from the house into the sheltering darkness of the gardens, strolling a pace or two then stopping to continue their exploratory kisses, limbs twining and parting and curving back together again at intervals until they came to a secluded glade at the edge of the lake.

Claudia switched off her thoughts and gave herself up to the lyrical pleasure of the senses. Evening spread a protective darkness over everything, wrapping them in its inky embrace. Beside them the waters lapped with a softly lulling sound, and from somewhere across the lake came a thin trail of melody as a pianist slowly picked out the notes of a popular song. Daniel held her face solemnly between his two hands and looked at her in the starlight for a long time, as if storing the moment in his memory for ever. Like the seventeen-year-old she once had been, in trusting this man and adoring him in the same way now, she felt as if time had spun them back to that point in the past from which the hand of fate had brought her, resisting, into his arms once more.

But now the time for resistance was thrown to the winds.

He lifted her protecting shirt, and groaned as he scooped her naked breasts against his mouth. Claudia gasped with pleasure, twisting against him and trembling with desire as his tongue ran over her naked skin. He dispensed with his own shirt and fumbled at the fastening of her jeans, as she slid down into the grass until she was lying full length under his warm body. The cool grass shocked her skin with its caress as he unpeeled her clothes, and she marvelled again at his masculine perfection as he shrugged rapidly out of his own clothes to join her in the grass. The soft, moist rasp of his tongue over the tensed muscles of her stomach made her shiver with expectation, and her fingers dug into the muscles of his back as his touch made her twist and moan against him. Endlessly kissing, with a strength of feeling to wipe out all the years lost to them, Claudia felt she was pouring out everything that had been in her heart. He held her carefully beneath him, every movement he made he was making for her, caressing her vulnerable body with a lingering sensuality so that she stretched pale and lovely in the grass, unashamed to reveal herself in nakedness before his gaze. Submitting so completely to the longing she read in his eyes seemed to be a promise for the future, but past and future no longer mattered when the present was full of Dan. His mouth followed a trail of instinctive desire along her body to the delicate flesh of her inner thighs. He searched out the sweet moist heat of her hunger, sucking her desire till it uncurled like a white hot flame.

Aroused beyond caution now, without thought of betrayal or deserting, she cried out at the first downward thrust as he came to her. Eyes shut tight, she arched against him, gasping in wonderment at the sensation of their two bodies moving together in a unison of ecstasy. She cried out as he transported her beyond the limits she had imagined, gasping and shuddering, and carried yet further until the final waves of passion engulfed them both and they clung together in the dying aftermath of a receding storm.

When she eventually opened her eyes, Daniel, sensitive to her slightest movement, raised his own head and looked down at her, his silvery eyes feathering softly like doves as he nuzzled her face with his own.

'When are you going to trust me enough to tell me the truth?' he murmured, cradling her in his arms, expecting no answer, for she was incapable of rational speech as yet. He fondled her until she drifted off into a half-sleep. For Claudia, it was a poignant conclusion to so much emotion to find that he held her close, one hand curving a breast, the other snaking through her hair, as if he would never stop touching her and would certainly never let her leave him.

As the night air chilled, she began to come back to life, remembering the questions she had still left unanswered, and tensing when she realised how foolish it was to hope that things had changed at all.

After this, there could be no more pretence at forgetting him. She would die with his name emblazoned on her heart. The thought made her tilt her head and give him a look that conveyed her change of mood.

'Cold?' he asked gently.

'A little,' she stalled. Then, as he skimmed her body with his hands, drawing her back under him, she struggled to sit up.

'No, Danny!' Rolling away from him, she evaded his outstretched arms and tried to make a grab for her shirt but, reading her intentions, he snatched it away from her.

'What's the matter?' He was sitting upright, peering at her intently through the darkness.

'It's nothing—I—felt cold,' she hedged. Then, more quickly, added, 'I just don't want to get too deeply involved with you. I don't *want* an affair. I couldn't face it when——'

'Hell's bells! Is that all you think I want from you?' He yanked at her shirt, pulling her off balance so that she fell down into the grass beside him. His free hand snaked round her shoulders, pulling her up close against his broad chest and pinning her there beneath him.

'I can have any number of affairs, if that's what I want. But it's not.'

'W-what else is there?' she whispered, crushed beneath him.

'What the hell do you think? I want what I should have had years ago . . . I want marriage to the mother of my son!'

CHAPTER TEN

FOR a moment, Claudia lay there in the grass, stunned into silence. Then, haltingly, as if the words came from far away, she asked, 'How—how long have you known? How did you find out?' Daniel's expression gave nothing away, and she searched frantically to see something in it that would give her a clue to what he felt. 'Daniel, don't look at me like that!' she cried out. 'When did you find out? Toby couldn't tell you. He thinks his father's dead ...' Realising how terrible that sounded, she added hastily, 'It just seemed easier to tell him that— oh, Daniel! Say something!'

'I will do if you'll calm down.' He pulled her closer towards him, but she couldn't tell whether it was a loving gesture, or merely designed to prevent her escape. Looking deep into her eyes, he asked, 'Why didn't you tell me at the time, for goodness' sake?'

'I did. I wrote to you. That was the letter I wrote.'

'And you thought I ignored it? You must have thought I was the lowest of the low—to get a girl pregnant and then do a bunk. I wonder you even managed to speak to me when we met up again——' He gazed searchingly into her eyes.

'I thought—I thought it was because I'd written in the letter that I was going to have an abortion. I thought you felt that allowed you to wash your hands of the whole business ...'

'But Toby?'

'It's all right. I changed my mind ...'

172

'Even though I apparently didn't care a damn?'

She nodded. How to explain the devastation of feeling when there was no reply—nails in the coffin? Then she became aware of the growing life, the realisation that it was Daniel growing inside her. That that was all she had of him. And, loving him as she still did, how she had clung on to this little there was—thankful, more than that, ragingly glad, despite the shame and anguish, that at least she had something of him, for ever, and always her own. She wanted to tell him how she had resolved to love him silently and faithfully through their child.

All she could say now was, 'It made me feel close to you.' Tears welled in her huge eyes. Love had seemed a futile emotion, but it had remained no matter how hard she had tried to root it out. One day, soon, she would tell him this.

Now, fear for the consequences shuddered through her. Desperately her eyes quested over his face for signs of the anger she expected.

'I was going to write to let you know when he was born ... but the more I thought about it, the more pointless it seemed. If you weren't interested the first time I wrote, you wouldn't be interested to hear you'd got a son. In fact,' she grimaced, 'I thought you'd be apalled. I just didn't know what to do.'

'So you did nothing.' His face had hardened. 'I can understand your predicament, but I don't see why you didn't let me know later, when you'd got over the trauma of those first few months. Didn't you give a single thought to Toby's future?'

'I decided then that I'd be the one to give him everything he needed—that he'd never want for anything.'

'Except a father ... My God, Claudia, you must have

seen me as some sort of monster!' His grip tightened bruisingly on her arm.

'No!' she exclaimed. 'I simply thought how reasonable it was—I thought, why should *he* care? I don't understand my own state of mind then, either,' she added, noting the puzzled look in his face. 'I felt it was my own stupid fault for getting pregnant in the first place. I should have been more careful——'

'So should I. Didn't it cross your mind that the blame was mine, too?'

'Not really,' she admitted. 'That summer I felt everything was my fault—Mother dying, Father going off with someone else, me lumbering you with fatherhood when you were only eighteen. The guilt was all mine. It drove me for years . . .'

'Poor idiot!' Daniel crushed her in his arms, stroking her hair over and over again. 'I can't bear the thought of you having to cope with all that by yourself. My poor, brave darling—you were only a child yourself. Who did you turn to?'

'No one,' she answered simply. 'When—when it was confirmed, I found the name of a nursing home for unmarried girls and went there.'

'So that's why you left no forwarding address?'

'I could hardly pass an address like that on! I felt so ashamed.'

'God!' He rose to his feet and began to pace restlessly about beneath the trees. The look he turned on her pierced her with the acuity of a sudden fury that seemed to be welling up inside him from some deep centre of his psyche. She crouched down in the grass, all her fears crowding back into her mind, sending her thoughts skittering in turmoil as she watched him.

Then her head rose. 'I'm glad I did it that way,' she

told him proudly. 'There was nothing else I could have done. You should thank me.'

'Thank you? For what?' he ground out, struggling to come to terms with his emotions.

'For saving you a lot of trouble—for not wrecking your university career——'

'Are you serious? I should *thank* you?' He seemed unable to speak, his anger boiling over. 'Thank you for letting my own son walk around for twelve years, thinking I was dead?' He gave a hollow laugh, and when she reached out to him he dashed her hands away.

It seemed as if her worst fears were materialising. This was what she had feared all along—the rejection of herself, the love she felt—and now it was happening before her eyes. 'Please, Daniel,' she croaked reaching out again.

'Don't touch me!' He jerked back out of range. 'You didn't give me a chance, did you? You could have contacted me at any time in the last twelve years. You could have told me the truth when we met again—but instead you hoarded him to you like a miser hoarding gold. What were you afraid of? That I would take him away from you?' He paused, gazing cruelly down at her. 'Maybe that's the best idea! I can give him so many things you can't—— despite your arrogance in assuming you can be everything to him.'

'Please don't say things like that, Daniel.'

'Damn you, I had a right to know about him! Who the hell were you to sit in judgement over me? What right had you to say I wasn't fit to hear the truth.'

'It wasn't like that!' Claudia cried out. But his anger was boiling over now.

'Are you only capable of thinking about your own feelings? What about Toby? Didn't you consider how he might feel, growing up with no knowledge of his own father? What lies did you tell him? And how do you think you're going to break the news to him now?'

The idea hadn't entered her head—so taken up with the effort at concealment had she been over these last few weeks when, for the first time, it had seemed as if the truth might leak out, that she hadn't given a thought to any further repercussions.

'I don't see why he need ever know if——' She was going to say, 'If you don't want him to,' but Daniel exploded at once.

'Woman—are you mad? Do you seriously imagine I'm going to let my own son slip through my fingers like a—like a discarded train ticket? He's flesh and blood, body and soul, he's a human being, damn you! A child you've sacrificed to preserve your own selfish image of sainted motherhood. He's got to know the truth!'

'Not now, Dan!' She started up, scrabbling at the buttons of her shirt, afraid that Daniel was going to go storming up to Toby's room now and confront him with the truth all at once.

'He's mine as much as yours. I'm going to make up for all the time we've lost.' He swerved violently towards the house and Claudia sprang after him, snatching convulsively at his arm. He shook her away and she fell back into the grass. Instead of striding off as he'd intended, he halted for a moment, and if she had been able to make out his features more clearly she would have seen the uncertainty he felt, the anguish for her still-living grief and the tenderness that love wrapped around her. But instead she felt his hands come down, pulling on the clothes that had been discarded in the transports of love, covering her, it seemed, as if her body, having sated him, now disgusted him with its nakedness. The years of telling herself that he couldn't care because of the original imagined rejection took over again, blunting her sensitivity to his actions, and distorting what they meant.

Daniel was torn by the desire to wrap her in his arms and sit there beside the lake's edge until the sun rose next morning, learning about her all over again, but a look at the dark hollows of her eyes stopped him, and instead he told her he would go back to the hotel.

'Get some sleep if you can,' he told her, emotion charging his voice, 'and we'll meet tomorrow. There are all kinds of legalities to discuss. Ramifications——' He ran a hand through his straight blond hair, the cool grey eyes picking out the signs of her obstinacy as he spoke. 'Do as I say. We both need time.'

As Claudia rose to her feet to stand beside him, her face came level with his mouth, but he resisted the impulse to smother her with kisses, and instead told her, 'Don't imagine things are going to go on as they have done. Everything's changed now. And you'd better believe it.'

Aware, not for the first time, of his practised authority, Claudia trembled with the effort to resist his attempt to take control. It had been too long a time that she had been in sole control of her own destiny for her to give up the reins so easily to someone else. His air of authority was a threat. It made her fight back blindly to hold on to what was hers.

'There's nothing to discuss. I think he's too young to be burdened with all this.'

'Will I be a burden to him?' Daniel snapped.

'It's too much for him,' she repeated stubbornly.

With no sense of conceding anything, he turned and started to walk towards the house.

'Keep away from him, Daniel. We've managed without you so far, and we can go on managing without you. So keep away!' she called after him.

Daniel didn't turn back. He knew what he was going to do, but tomorrow was the time to talk sense into her. And besides, he himself needed time. Fatherhood had been a concept quite outside his image of himself. It was only when he had been out in the boat with Toby that the truth had dawned on him—the similarities between them were striking—and there had been that photograph in the flat, too—the ten-year-old in it had had an uncanny resemblance to himself at ten—he'd thought it odd at the time, but then forgotten it till now. Fatherhood had all the allure of novelty. But hidden dangers, unknown responsibilities lurked to. It was all a confusion of thought, expectation and emotion. He needed time, whether she did or not.

Claudia had taken his peremptory tones to mean masculine arrogance, insensitivity to the pain his threat to tell Toby had aroused. She ran alongside him as soon as she had slipped back into her jeans and put on her shoes.

'You can decide what you like! *I'm* his mother. It's been me fighting for survival all these years by myself—you can keep out of it, Daniel Sinnington. You damn well keep away from us! We don't want you!'

For a moment he looked back at her. In the darkness her eyes were like two empty black holes in the ghostlike face. He felt her will building up against him, but he decided to let it go for now, confident that in the morning she would feel differently.

As she watched him disappear round a corner of the house, she silently vowed, 'You'll *never* take him from me!' Toby had been central to her life for so long. He *was* her life. Without him, she would have no heart left. She would become a hollow shell.

All night she plotted feverishly. What could she do if Daniel found some legal right of custody and took Toby away? Discarding that thought—for wouldn't she fight him through all the courts in the land?—she thought of all the other ways he could deprive her of her son. Kidnap? She shuddered. With his wealth, what could stop him from whisking Toby off to some secret destination abroad? Agitation spread its swift poison through her mind. She would be powerless to stop him. This would be obvious to Daniel himself. Was that what it would come to if she resisted him in his designs?

She could pre-empt him by hiding Toby until she had had a proper talk to him—warned him of the dangers that lay in wait from any contact with him. But to do that she would have to tell Toby the truth. No matter how she looked at it, she was brought back to this one ineluctable fact.

The thought of plucking up the nerve to go to him and say, 'Well, actually, what I've always told you about your father was nothing but lies,' made her recoil. What had started out as a young girl's desperate attempts to survive as best she could, had turned with the passage of years into a web of deceit.

Knowing that it was the only thing to do—that Toby actually had a right to know that his father was very much alive, she resolved to do it first thing in the morning. Then she would take Toby safely off to school. He would be out of Daniel's reach there. It would give her time to decide what to do next. And surely Daniel too, after time for thought, would come round to a more reasonable response? Weekend visits would surely be the most he would contemplate, once the matter had sunk in properly? He would surely see sense and quietly fade from the scene.

The image of Daniel fading quietly from anything was vaguely preposterous, but she clung to the fantasy all night, as if by visualising it strongly enough she could make it happen.

Next morning Toby bounded out early. Claudia's exhausted night-time ruminations had sent her into a dreamless sleep long after dawn, so that it was only the sound of his crashing around in the bathroom that dragged her to the surface. He was tucking into cornflakes in the kitchen by the time she caught up with him.

'Come on, Mum. I'm going to be late back. I don't want to lose my early leave next weekend!'

'Toby——' she launched herself into the distasteful business straight away '—I have something very——' she paused '—well, disturbing to tell you.'

She sat down next to him on the kitchen bench, and put an arm round his shoulders.

'You're not ill are you, Mum?' Concern showed itself on his clean-cut face. He was like a miniature version of Daniel—how could she have hoped to conceal the truth?

'No, it's something to do with you,' she said carefully.

'Oh lor, what've I done now?' He furrowed his brow.

'Listen to me, Toby darling, please don't jump to conclusions——' She nearly added, 'like your father', but stopped herself in time. His big blue eyes were fixed on hers, mirrors almost of her own. 'I've always let you believe that your daddy was dead, because a long, long time ago something happened that meant we—I—we lost touch with each other.'

'Like a quarrel or a war or something?'

She nodded. 'Something neither of us could help—a misunderstanding . . . He actually never knew he had a baby. I—I thought it best never to tell him. But now,' she added in a rush, 'he's found out and he wants you to know——'

'I won't have to go and live with him, will I?' asked Toby anxiously. Then, before she could allay his fears, he added, 'Though if he lives somewhere interesting, it'd be OK to visit for holidays. Lots of the lads do that when their folks divorce . . .' He gave her a disarming smile. 'When do I get to meet him?'

'Actually, you've already met . . .'

Toby puzzled for a moment, then started to smile, and before she could add anything he beamed, 'If you're going to say it's Dan, I'm going to give you a big kiss!'

'Oh, Toby, don't you mind?'

'It *is*! It's Dan, isn't it? I *knew* it was! It is, isn't it, Mum?'

She nodded, too full of emotion to trust herself to speak.

'I *told* you he was OK!'

'Toby!' She crunched him up against her. 'You knew, did you?' Hot tears sprang into her eyes, and she had to bury her face in his fragrant hair to hide the sudden uprush of relief that the truth was out at last.

'Of course I knew. Didn't you?' he asked innocently.

'Of course I did, you idiot!' She realised that at some time he would work it all out, but it was a joy to know that he was undisturbed by the news. It hadn't undermined his sense of identity and, rather than sink in his estimation, she seemed to have gone up—by providing such a popular figure for the role!

'Come on, we'll be late!' Catching sight of the time,

he jumped to his feet, already mentally back in the more real word of school.

'There is one thing,' Claudia said as he fastened up his blazer. 'We may not be able to see too much of Dan. He's——' She paused. How could she explain to a twelve-year-old the fear Daniel's words last night had aroused about losing him altogether?

'. . . he's very busy,' she finished lamely.

'Well, that's OK. I'm busy, too!' grinned Toby as he turned to the door. Astonished that the first hurdle had been surmounted so easily, Claudia walked almost light-heartedly to the car.

As she drove into town, the thought passed swiftly through her mind that it might even be easy to tell Susie the whole story now—she had worn a very thoughtful expression the other day when the topic of Toby's birthday had cropped up. She had coupled it almost casually with the observation that Claudia was lucky to have had him in her teens, so that she was still young now that Toby himself was entering his teens. There had been an odd, dawning look in her eyes as she spoke.

Daniel had said one thing to Claudia that she had pushed to the back of her mind because his reaction to the discovery of his true relationship with Toby had knocked everything else to kingdom come. And that was when he had said he wanted to marry her.

With an effort she recalled his exact words. 'I want marriage to the mother of my son.' Not, 'I want to marry *you*, Claudia.' In other words, she could have been anybody. Anybody, she registered silently, he had happened to have a child by—the partner of a one-night fling, anybody. It was his sense of honour, of the rightness of things, that had made him mention the word marriage at all. It was obvious that a man like

Daniel would believe that, whatever his own feelings on the matter, to have a son inevitably implied the existence of a wife. Such a marriage, she mused in the solitude of her office that morning, would be a loveless convention and nothing more. She shuddered at the thought. Bad enough to be tied to any man for life without love. But to be shackled by marriage bonds to an indifferent husband one happened to be crazy about would be a living hell.

Daniel's phone call came half-way through the morning. Prepared for it as she was, his voice sent random tremors of apprehension shaking through her body.

'Lunch time,' he stated briskly, brooking no excuses. 'Come over here at one. Make sure you have the afternoon free. This may take time.'

'But I can't just——'

'Yes, you can. Be on time.'

She barely had time to register her annoyance at his high-handed attitude before the phone was slapped down at the other end.

At five minutes to one Claudia stormed through reception and burst into his office unannounced.

'It's no good! You're not taking him away. He's happy where he is. He has friends, love, security. You dare spoil it for him and I'll—I'll kill you! I mean it! Just you dare——'

'Hey, hey! Steady!' Before she could stop him, Daniel stood up from behind his desk where she had surprised him and strode towards her, sweeping her hard into his arms.

Mesmerised by his sudden proximity, she gazed blankly at the lips that hovered just above her own, and willed him not to kiss her. If he did, all would be lost and she would find herself agreeing to anything, well, almost anything, he might suggest.

'First,' he began, 'I have no intention of moving Toby from school. He seems wildly happy there. Second——' He paused.

'Yes?' she prompted, scarcely daring to breathe when he didn't continue.

'Second——' he repeated, his expression suddenly dazed, as if he had lost the thread. 'Oh, what the hell, Claudia?' he murmured against the side of her face, running his hands roughly over her already yielding body, 'I love you. Does anything else matter?'

She felt the swimmy feeling that his nearness always brought begin to take over with a vengeance, blunting her rational protests and annulling all the objections she'd had to this summons into his presence. With an effort she tried to focus on what he had been trying to say. 'You were so angry with me last night——' she prompted. In a world that had suddenly become misty, that much at least was certain. She shuddered now at the memory.

'I was—I'm not going to deny it. I felt——' He closed his eyes, as if trying to focus on something that had happened a long time in the past. All his attention seemed to be fixed on sampling the texture of her skin just below her left earlobe.

She tried to move away, but something invisible, with the power of a magnet, seemed to drag her back. 'Daniel,' she chided, 'please pay attention and finish what you were saying.'

'Yes, my darling,' he murmured, lapsing into silence again while his tongue made little trills and runs over her neck.

When the intercom buzzed, he didn't seem to hear it at first, and Claudia herself was so wrapped up in watching the way he eventually leaned over to flick it on that she scarcely registered the words that came over.

He knocked the switch back and caught her by the wrist, hauling her up close again. 'We have to go. They're ready,' he murmured absently. Still preoccupied with the excursions of his lips against the side of her face, he none the less pushed her gently towards the door and, before she knew what was happening, she found herself being hurried, still wrapped in his arms, across the lawn at the back of the hotel towards the scarlet and white helicopter that was sitting there like some huge bird of prey. Its engines were already idling, and Claudia felt her face blanch as all her nightmares about Toby being kidnapped came flooding back. But what if, instead of Toby, she herself . . .?

'Dan!' she protested, stopping suddenly and digging in her heels. 'I don't want——'

'Don't be scared,' he reassured fondly. 'I want to show you where we'll live. See if you like it——'

'Live?'

'If I could have fixed a marriage licence overnight I would have . . .' He laughed, holding her in his arms as the engines began to roar around them. 'Come on, it'll only take a few minutes.'

When they were seated safely inside he said, 'By the look on your face you'd think you were being kidnapped!'

Ruefully, she confessed, 'I was awake all night with two worries chasing each other round and round in my head . . . you seemed so angry when you left, I really thought you meant to take Toby away from me.'

'Tug-of-love child? Toby?' And after a pause he added incredulously, 'Me? Claudia, how could you?'

'It seems stupid now,' she shamefacedly admitted.

'Night terrors. You know what they're like.'

'And the other one?'

'What? Oh, that! It was because of what you said about Toby. I'd no idea how he'd take it——'

'And how did he take it?' broke in Daniel anxiously, his face serious at once.

'It can be summed up in two words—nonchalant delight,' she smiled softly. 'I think he sees me as Mother Christmas giving him the best present he could possibly imagine.'

She noted the look of relief in his eyes. He took her hand.

'I only want what you want for him, and what he wants himself.' Daniel paused. 'I didn't know whether I had the right to come crashing into your lives, when you'd managed so well without me.' He gripped her hand a little harder. 'I must have been dumb not to guess the truth outright when I saw his photograph in your flat. But he looked older than he is. It didn't make sense. I convinced myself that it was a nephew or something. But, Claudia, I mean it. I won't change things if you don't want me to—but, hell, I can't help feeling that I've somehow got to try to make up to you both for not being around when you really needed me.' The expression on his face was still uncertain, and she leaned forward to rest her cheek softly against his.

'We need you, Dan. Both of us need you.' It was her turn to look anxious. 'The thing is, if we have to manage alone again, we will. I'd hate it if you felt you had to——' She bit her lip.

'What? Make an honest woman of you?' As he laughed, she felt all the doubts drain from him, and her own misgivings vanished at the same time. He stroked her hair as he went on, 'I was angry last night because I felt sorry for *myself*—for being deprived of him and of you, through all those years.'

She slipped easily into the crook of his arms as the helicopter gave a lurch. It was already coming in to land, scudding past the tops of some trees and beginning to circle over a rambling grey stone house set amid a sea of green.

'There it is!' He pointed. 'Think you'll like it?'

'Darling, anywhere you are.' Then she peered down through the window. 'It looks like paradise.' Her eyes mirrored her feelings. 'Paradise below and heaven here above.'

He spoke through the speaker to the pilot in the cockpit. 'Once more round the park before lunch.' Then, turning to her, his lips sought hers.

'Oughtn't we to——' Claudia broke off with a little gasp as he began to caress her.

'Oughtn't we to continue where we left off thirteen years ago?' he suggested huskily.

Her anxious look changed to a smile as she drew him down to her. Now at last she could accept what she had tried in vain to deny, for he was what he had always been——impossible to forget.

The Perfect Gift.

Four new exciting novels from Mills and Boon:

SOME SORT OF SPELL – by Frances Roding
– An enchantment that couldn't last or could it?

MISTRESS OF PILLATORO – by Emma Darcy
– The spectacular setting for an unexpected romance.

STRICTLY BUSINESS – by Leigh Michaels
– highlights the shifting relationship between friends.

A GENTLE AWAKENING – by Betty Neels
– demonstrates the truth of the old adage 'the way to a man's heart…'

Make Mother's Day special with this perfect gift.
Available February 1988. Price: £4.80

From: Boots, Martins, John Menzies, W H Smith,
Woolworths and other paperback stockists.

In a Swiss bank vault lurks a 30 year old secret.

When Ashley Wakefield and her twin brother David learnt that they had inherited an enormous trust fund, little did they know that they would be swept into a whirlwind of intrigue, suspense, danger and romance. Events stretching back to the 1956 Hungarian uprising unfolded once Ashley was photographed wearing her magnificent gems.

Published March 1988   Price £2.95

WORLDWIDE

Available from Boots, Martins, John Menzies, W H Smith, Woolworth and other paperback stockists.

ROMANCE

Next month's romances from Mills & Boon

Each month, you can choose from a world of variety in romance with Mills & Boon. These are the new titles to look out for next month.

MY BROTHER'S KEEPER Emma Goldrick
DARK LUCIFER Stephanie Howard
TARIK'S MOUNTAIN Dana James
PAYMENT IN LOVE Penny Jordan
TAKEOVER Madeleine Ker
CLOSE COLLABORATION Leigh Michaels
THE COURSE OF TRUE LOVE Betty Neels
FORTUNES OF LOVE Jessica Steele
MISTAKEN WEDDING Sally Wentworth
SAVAGE HUNGER Sara Wood
***RIDER OF THE HILLS** Miriam Macgregor
***HEART'S TREASURE** Annabel Murray
***A GOLDEN TOUCH** Mary Moore
***ANOTHER EDEN** Nicola West

Buy them from your usual paperback stockist, or write to: Mills & Boon Reader Service, P.O. Box 236, Thornton Rd, Croydon, Surrey CR9 3RU, England. Readers in Southern Africa — write to: Independent Book Services Pty, Postbag X3010, Randburg, 2125, S. Africa.

*These four titles are available from Mills & Boon Reader Service.

Mills & Boon
the rose of romance

AND THEN HE KISSED HER...

This is the title of our new venture — an audio tape designed to help you become a successful Mills & Boon author!

In the past, those of you who asked us for advice on how to write for Mills & Boon have been supplied with brief printed guidelines. Our new tape expands on these and, by carefully chosen examples, shows you how to make your story come alive. And we think you'll enjoy listening to it.

You can still get the printed guidelines by writing to our Editorial Department. But, if you would like to have the tape, please send a cheque or postal order for £4.95 (which includes VAT and postage) to:

VAT REG. No. 232 4334 96

AND THEN HE KISSED HER...

To: Mills & Boon Reader Service, FREEPOST, P.O. Box 236, Croydon, Surrey CR9 9EL.

Please send me _____ copies of the audio tape. I enclose a cheque/postal order*, crossed and made payable to Mills & Boon Reader Service, for the sum of £_____. *Please delete whichever is not applicable.

Signature _____

Name (BLOCK LETTERS) _____

Address _____

_____ Post Code _____